BOYS OF SUMMER

RHIAN CAHILL

Boys of Summer
By Rhian Cahill

For more information visit:
www.rhiancahill.com

BONDI BEACH BOYS

Thanks to Selena for being the "ideas" person and asking me to take part in her brilliance. For all the women who have ever stretched out on a beach and watched the scenery go by. And for those who haven't, here's a snippet of what you're missing. To Mr. C. you're all the scenery I need.

1

PIPER PUSHED through the glass door and sucked in a blast of hot air like walking into the bowels of hell, but she wasn't going back inside the air-conditioned interior of the cafe for anything. Not until she'd had her daily dose of what she'd affectionately dubbed her *Bondi Beach Boys*.

She smiled at the nickname she'd given them. Having lived in Sydney for only ten months, she hadn't fully understood the appeal of sitting by Bondi Beach on a stinking hot day, but summer was rapidly becoming her favorite time of year.

A waitress delivered her fresh-squeezed juice, and Pip thanked the girl without taking her eyes off the view. Picking up the ice-cold glass, she brought it to her lips. The heady mix of sweet aromas filled her nose, and the freshly blended flavors of mango and banana exploded on her tongue. Still, her eyes remained glued to the sight in front of her. A shiver skipped down her spine, and it had nothing to do with the chunk of ice she sucked on.

Bodies of all shapes and sizes, in all manner of dress, littered the hot sand. Kids with buckets and spades built sandcastles by the water's edge. Teenagers in long, baggy shorts played a game of volleyball, kicking up arcs of golden spray. Women in skimpy bikinis lay on towels, glistening under the scorching sun. But Pip came for the men.

There were all kinds. Young, old, skinny and fat, some in Speedos with bronzed bodies worth drooling over; they were all there. Though none of those were the attraction for her. Two men in particular drew her gaze day after day, week after week. With her sunglasses shielding her eyes, she turned a little to the right and looked her fill.

Bronze hair and skin sparkled under the hot sun. Long, tanned limbs rippled with muscle as the sun god they were attached to reached up and removed the surfboard from the roof rack of the sporty, black sedan. She licked her lips. Tingling with the urge to run her tongue over every inch of the bare torso, Piper's mouth had gone bone dry, the ice cube long since melted away. Her gaze skipped further to the right to find the second most glorious sight in the world.

His sleek muscles were dusted with dark hair, and the smooth skin holding it all together had to be what people referred to as a Mediterranean complexion. No less appealing than the golden specimen on the other side of the vehicle, he made her heart race and her palms sweat. Together they were a sexy temptation a nun would be hard pressed to refuse. Piper sighed and took another sip of her drink.

She watched them as they got ready, prepping their boards, throwing towels around their shoulders, and locking up the car. The blond picked up a backpack and turned toward the waves. For long moments, Piper admired the shift of muscles along backbones made for licking. Her temperature, already hot from the sweltering summer weather, went up a couple of degrees. Arousal swirled low in her abdomen, the once gentle stir now a churning whirlpool, and her chest rose and fell with her harsh breaths.

Today was no different from any of the others in the past few weeks. Her *Bondi Beach Boys* surveyed the waves as they rolled onto the sand of Sydney's most famous beach. She studied them—her boys, not the waves. Their wind-tossed hair: one dark blond with golden streaks, the other black as night. Their smooth backs and narrow hips, miles of leg beneath brightly colored shorts. But the gorgeous asses hidden under the quick-dry material drew Piper's eyes the most.

She'd always been a butt girl. Something about a tight pair of cheeks just did it for her. Pip wasn't worried what covered a guy's rear end, but she had to admit to being partial to jeans before this summer. Now though... Now she was a converted woman.

Absolutely nothing compared to a set of firm buns wrapped in wet board shorts. No siree, nothing better. What a shame she wouldn't be here to see them all wet and shiny when they came back to the car.

Her normal routine had to be rearranged for a meeting with potential new clients, and there was no way she was going to risk blowing this interview. She really didn't need to go back over the designs—she'd been up til three a.m. making sure they were perfect—but she couldn't help wanting to give it one more look with fresh eyes before the meeting.

This job could be the big break that allowed her to quit her part-time cleaning gig and purchase that new software and hard drive she had her eye on. Tipping up her glass, she drank the last of her juice as her boys made their way down onto the sand.

Piper grabbed her bag and stood. Having paid for her drink when she ordered, she made her way between the tables to the sidewalk. The blond dropped the backpack and his towel, and jogged to the water's edge. His friend followed at a more leisurely pace. She paused, watching them as they dropped their boards to the water and lowered their buff bodies to the fiberglass lengths. They paddled out, ducking under the waves and giving her one final glimpse of taut butt muscles before she forced herself to leave. With a sigh, Pip turned and headed home.

SAM SCANNED THE TABLES, searching for the brunette. Disappointment surged when she proved to be nowhere in sight. He and Nate had gotten used to seeing her the past few weeks. Dropping his bag, he leaned his board against the car and knelt down to retrieve the car keys from the bottom of the backpack. He pressed the button to unlock the doors. Nate stepped up next to him, and Sam noticed his friend doing exactly what he'd done a moment before.

"Damn. She's gone."

"Yeah." Sam glanced at his wristwatch. "Looks like we've all got somewhere to be this morning."

"Bugger. If I'd known that I'd have hung around longer before hitting the waves."

Sam smiled. He'd had the same idea. He really wanted to find out who she was. The need to know her had been building for days—weeks—and that morning, when they'd pulled up and seen her walking into the cafe, he'd decided to introduce himself. Another look at his watch told him they didn't have time to dwell on her early disappearance.

"Tomorrow, I think I'll skip the surf and have a smoothie instead." He grinned over his board at Nate and tossed him the keys.

His mate snatched the keys out of the air one-handed. "Not without me, you're not."

They locked their boards into the racks and climbed into the car. As Nate started the engine, air blasted through the vents. The stale, hot gust slammed into Sam's face before the air-conditioner kicked in to cool it. Maybe he should offer to teach her to surf when he talked to her. No doubt about it, he'd be making a new friend before lunchtime tomorrow.

Five minutes of fighting with traffic and they were pulling into the underground garage beneath their house and office. He and Nate ran their business from the first floor of the three-story refurbished home. Sam had a soft spot in his heart for the place, their second fixer-upper. The first had netted them enough profit that turning this one over hadn't been a necessity, and both agreed it made a good base for their growing business.

Nate parked the car and got out, heading straight for the door leading into the basement and the spiral staircase to the other levels, leaving Sam to clean the boards and put them away. By the time he finished and headed upstairs to shower, he passed Nate coming back down in their usual business attire, cargo pants and polo shirt with the company logo over the left-hand breast pocket.

The emblem was the only thing they'd requested the new web designer keep, and Sam looked forward to their meeting, anxious to see what the guy had come up with. He looked forward to not having to update the site in the future too.

With the company growing, they found it more and more difficult to keep up with all aspects of the business, and like some of the actual labor, they were hiring someone else to oversee their website. The guy they'd sold their last house to recommended the designer. Jeff's website was brilliant, and Sam thought it took someone special to make a dentist's online presence look good.

He tossed the wet towels in the laundry as he strolled past; he'd throw them in the washer after their meeting. He walked through the bedroom and headed straight for the bathroom. Stripping out of his shorts, he stepped into the large shower recess, the supersized area one of his biggest indulgences. Multiple jets angled to spray every part of the body with steaming water, and an alcove with a bench seat and a glass wall looked out over the ocean, all pleasure for the senses. Sam reached for the soap and lathered it in his hands.

"Need some help with that?" Nate asked.

"I'd love some, but we don't have time for that right now." Sam eyed the bulge in the front of Nate's pants. "What's got you all hot and bothered?"

"The brunette."

Sam arched a brow. "Really?"

Nate laughed. "Like I don't know you've been jerking off to the image of her in your head for the last few weeks."

Sighing, Sam turned under the spray to rinse off. His friend was right; the little brunette had gotten under his skin in a big way. And considering he didn't even know her name, never mind the color of her eyes, he was probably in big trouble.

"Don't stress it. We're in the same boat." Nate held out a towel. "Tomorrow we get to know her."

"Tomorrow," Sam agreed, the word a promise and a prayer.

NATE MADE his way back to their office. He'd already rung Burt, their foreman, and knew the Baker Street job continued to be on schedule, he'd spoken to Emily at the bank about their overdraft, and he'd cleared the conference table ready for the meeting with the web designer. All that remained to do was to start the coffee. Sam walked in, his blond hair still damp from the shower, and Nate glanced at the clock to see if they had time for a quickie. They had thirty minutes until show time, plenty to get his rocks off and remove the raw edge he currently rode.

"Drop your pants." He growled the words as he stalked across the room.

"Like that, is it?" Sam smiled with that know-it-all grin that always got Nate's demanding nature riled up.

"Yes. Drop 'em."

Sam turned his back, pushed his hips back, and wiggled his ass. "Make me."

Nate almost crash-tackled him to the ground. In record time, he had the button and fly of Sam's pants undone and the gorgeous cock hiding inside in his hand. He stroked hard, the way Sam liked it. A moan slipped from Sam's throat and Nate ground his erection into the curve of his friend's ass.

"I need..."

"I know." Sam broke from his grasp and pushed his pants down. He always knew how to soothe the savage inside Nate. They'd been friends long before they'd become lovers, and Nate still thanked the woman who'd shown them this other side of themselves. Fumbling with his belt, he struggled to control his trembling fingers.

"Jeez, she's really got you on edge." Sam brushed Nate's hands aside and dispensed with Nate's trousers.

"Totally."

"Good. We're in the same place then."

"No offense, but I'm gonna pretend you're her when I bury my cock in your ass."

"None taken." Sam slid a condom down Nate's length, sending fire into Nate's balls and a shudder up his spine. "I'll be doing the same when I fuck you."

Nate laughed as he shoved Sam over to the table. "Hold on."

Sam leaned forward, thrust his ass toward Nate, and gripped the table in front of them. Lining himself up with Sam's puckered hole, Nate slid forward, his mate's ass easily taking his thick cock all the way to the balls. He pulled out, pushed in. Hard and fast. Slam after slam, his thighs hit the back of Sam's as he fucked him until the heat in his balls boiled over and he came in a rush.

"Agh..." The cry tore from his lips and he collapsed on Sam's back.

"No time for rest yet." Sam stood up, dislodging Nate from his resting place.

Nate pulled his spent cock from Sam's still clenching hole. His legs were like rubber, so he turned and leaned his butt on the table. He wrapped his fingers around his softening length and removed the used condom.

"Too tired to stand?" Sam had the know-it-all grin going on again as he rolled a condom down his cock. "I can work with that."

He grabbed Nate's ankles off the floor and pushed them up, making him lie back on the table. Nate's legs were tangled in his pants, but that didn't stop Sam. He just pushed until Nate kissed his own knees and Sam could step into Nate's waiting body. The position put his ass in line with Sam's cock and he soon found himself on the receiving end of a good, hard and fast fuck. Muscles stretched to fit the thick rod driving into him. His sated cock was rejuvenated by the slide of Sam's erection over his prostate. Much more and he'd be coming again.

As if he'd read his mind, Sam wrapped a hand around Nate's rapidly hardening cock and pumped, the harshness of the caress designed to drive him over the edge. Nate might be demanding and rough at times, but Sam liked to prove he could take him down a peg or two, and much to Nate's pleasure, it seemed as though Sam was of a mind to do just that.

His friend slowed the thrust of his cock, but sped up his hand. Nate shoved his pants to his ankles and widened his knees, made it easier for Sam to wank him off. With blinding speed, Nate raced to his second release. Cum flowed from his cock, spurting onto both their stomachs as Sam leaned into him.

"Done now?" Sam asked.

Nate's hands shook where he held his knees against his shoulders. The tremors of his orgasm continued to roll through him, but he managed a nod.

With his hands now palming the back of Nate's thighs, Sam proceeded to fuck him. Driving deep, ramming hard, he took what he needed until he shouted out with his own climax.

2

PIPER STARED out of the side window of the taxi. "Are you sure this is the address I gave you?"

"Yep, fifty-two Wentworth."

"Fifty-two Wentworth Street, Dover Heights?"

"What? You think I don't know my way around Sydney?"

The slip of paper Pip had written the address on trembled in her hand. "But it's a house."

"Look, lady, it's the address you gave me. Either pay up the twenty-six seventy-five you owe me and get out, or tell me where else you wanna go."

Startled, she turned to face the man. Piper saw the exasperation lining his dark face and quickly reached into her purse for money. Thrusting out three ten dollar notes, she grabbed her portfolio with one hand and yanked on the door handle with the other. No sooner had she exited the taxi and shut the door than the driver tore off in reverse. He backed into the driveway next door, then drove off down the street with a squeal of tires. Sighing, Pip turned to look at the multi-story dwelling behind her.

Could she have written down the wrong address? She shook her head. No, she remembered checking—again—the details in the email before leaving home. Looking up, she counted three levels, possibly one below ground as well, because the drive sloped sharply down to meet a wide metal door not unlike those seen in parking garages. With the large expanse of mirrored glass walls and the two huge smoked glass doors, it could pass as a small office building, but Piper didn't think that's what it was.

For some reason, it gave off the vibe of home. The contemporary design was the furthest thing from a homely cottage and white picket fence you could get, but Piper couldn't deny the feeling of welcome the property gave her. Brushing her knee-length skirt down with one hand, she assured herself of her professional attire and began the walk to the front doors. Her low wedge heels landed on the paved walkway with a thudding rhythm that matched her heartbeat.

She was nervous. A lot rode on landing this client. Piper thought the job she'd done on their web redesign had turned out good—no, brilliant. Probably her best work to date. But that was subjective, and ultimately it came down to the client's happiness. Two wide steps led to the massive front doors. Her reflection bounced back at her, and once again she ran a hand over her skirt, her blouse, and finally the length of her hair. Her dead-straight locks were simple and manageable; Pip had never been a high-maintenance kind of girl. Growing up with three older brothers had seen to that.

Standing tall, she gripped her portfolio in one hand, her palm sweating around the leather strap. Piper took a deep breath and let it out slowly. Now or never. Reaching out, she pushed the intercom button and heard the musical doorbell echo behind those smooth glass panels. She tried not to fidget, but her feet shuffled on the tile stoop anyway. Her breathing came in short, shallow bursts and Pip wondered if she might hyperventilate right there at the door.

She needn't have been concerned—her shortness of breath was nothing compared to the complete lack of it when the doors swung open to reveal none other than her golden *Bondi Beach Boy*. She stared at him, her mouth gaping open, and thought perhaps she was dreaming. Maybe she'd fallen asleep on her lumpy, second-hand couch at home and hadn't even left for her business meeting yet.

Spellbound, she could only look. Her eyes felt huge, and she could feel them drying up as her lids refused to drop.

They stood there, held in some kind of trance, his facial expression reminding her of when one of her brothers had punched another in the stomach.

"Melted chocolate."

His words made no sense. "What?"

"The color of your eyes. Soft and warm, like melted Cadbury chocolate."

"Excuse me?" Piper struggled to follow the conversation, if that's what it could be called.

"Sam, what the hell are you..."

And there he is, Beach Boy number two.

What little air had been left in her lungs was sucked out. Standing in front of her were both her *Bondi Beach Boys*. From a distance, they were gorgeous. Up close they were devastating. Her body tingled and her vision had sparkly little stars dancing around. Passing out on their front step suddenly seemed a definite possibility. She swayed forward, but before she face planted on the tile beneath her feet, strong arms wrapped around her shoulders and dragged her into the house.

"Christ!"

"Get her inside. It's too damn hot out there."

"Are you alright?"

"Bring her into the office. I'll grab some water."

Piper heard the doors close with a whoosh behind her, heard the words of concern, but couldn't decipher them. Her heart thudded against her ribs and the beat of her blood pounded in her ears, each thump a solid whack to her nervous system. She'd never fainted in her life and couldn't believe she was going to do it now when she'd come to pitch a job.

Golden Boy slid an arm around her back and his other behind her knees. A squeak of protest left her throat as he hoisted her against his hard chest and walked deeper into the house.

Giving in to the comforting warmth of the arms surrounding her, she rested her head on his shoulder and let him carry her away. Her eyelids drifted down, and Piper thought it ironic that now they worked when she wanted desperately to see everything around her. He placed her in a butter-soft leather chair, the cushion under her butt cupping her curves in its supple grip. One of them pushed a glass of water in front of her face and pried her portfolio bag from her hand. Someone wiggled Piper's purse, still draped over her shoulder, out of the way too.

"Drink some water."

She raised her eyelids and stared at the man crouched at her feet, his dark hair standing at odd angles like he'd run his fingers through it a few times. Her palms itched to reach out and smooth down the chaotic spikes. Instead she reached for the glass and brought the cold rim to her lips. Icy water splashed into her mouth and down over her chin and fingers as her hand trembled.

"Here, let me help."

Dark, thick fingers covered hers, held the glass to her lips, and tipped it up. As the soothing liquid flowed over her tongue, it sent a shiver down her spine. She took small sips, even though she wanted to guzzle every last drop in an attempt to douse the fire blazing inside her.

Piper used the time to settle her nerves, to bring her breath and heart back under control, and to brush away some of the fog in her mind. When she'd consumed half the contents, she pushed the drink away, his hand still wrapped around hers. With a sigh she leaned back into the chair.

"Feeling better?"

Piper blinked. She licked her lips and tried to form a word, but her tongue stuck to the roof of her mouth and the word wouldn't come out, so she nodded instead.

As Piper's faculties started to work again, she kept looking between them. This close, they were even more handsome. The blond's eyes were as blue as the summer sky. Pip wanted to stare into them forever, but she dragged her gaze to the dark god still holding her drink and studied his face. The curve of his jaw was sprinkled with black stubble—he'd obviously skipped shaving. Eyes black as coal stared back at her, and she wanted to squirm in her seat under his heated gaze but somehow managed to stay still. She lowered her eyes, and for the first time since the door had opened, Piper saw the logo on their matching shirts.

"You're S & N Construction?" *Oh my God! It can't be. Why did the world have to be so cruel?* There was no way she could do anything about her attraction to either of them if they were clients.

"And you're P. Doyle." The blond pointed to her portfolio with its embossed gold letters, a gift from her parents when she'd left home the previous autumn.

"Piper Doyle," she answered, even though it hadn't really been a question.

The dark one extended his right hand. "Well, it's lovely to meet you, Piper. I'm Nathan, but everyone calls me Nate."

"And I'm Sam."

Piper didn't know which hand to shake first. She chose Nate's hand only because he'd offered first. As his warm skin connected with hers, Pip jolted with a shock of awareness. A sizzle zipped up her arm, leaving goose bumps in its wake. Pulling her hand from his, she held her breath and took Sam's. Again she received a zap when their flesh touched. These two men had her buzzing with arousal, and she could do nothing but grin and bear it. With a sigh, she let go.

"It's nice to meet you both." In an attempt to regain some dignity and push her wayward hormones out of the way, Piper sucked in a deep breath and straightened in her chair. "I apologize for my..." She struggled to find the right words.

"There's nothing to be sorry for," Nate said. "It's one hell of a day out there. Even the devil himself would find it hard to keep his feet under him in these temperatures."

"Well, I'd still like to start this meeting over again, with a little more professionalism this time."

"If this is what you've worked up for our website, you could turn up in a clown suit and still get the job."

Piper looked up to find Sam leafing through the file of printouts she'd put together of the design for S & N Construction. Nate stood and stepped over beside Sam. They flipped from page to page, pointing at parts they liked. The knot in her stomach eased as the two men appraised her work with smiles. Pip pushed to her feet and brushed her clothes straight before picking up her bag and pulling out her laptop.

Placing the computer on the large table to her left, Pip switched it on before turning back to the two men still studying her work. Confidence flowed through her, making her tense muscles loosen and enthusiasm grow. She stepped over to take the folder from Sam's hands.

"If you'll please sit down, I'll run through the demonstration of your site so you'll be able to see how it will work once it's live on your server."

"And you're able to take care of all that? The changeover?" Nate asked.

"Yes, once you give me the go-ahead, I'll change to the new design and maintain the site from then on."

Adrenaline pumped through her; the usual thrill of showing a client a new design had an extra edge this morning. Her attraction to the two men drove the normal desire to do a good job higher, amplified it. Piper slipped into work mode and demonstrated the online shop she'd created especially for them. Their business was unique, and therefore the way customers came to them would be too. Lost in the world of her own creation, she didn't notice the time, but couldn't help but notice the two men whose attention she held.

Their warmth surrounded her. Their scent filled her—fresh soap and man. Encircled in a cocoon created by Sam and Nate, she should have felt uncomfortable—they were potent, powerful men—but Pip found herself leaning into each of them as they talked about the new design and how long it would take to go live.

The excitement of landing the job arced through her. Once they signed the contract, the job was hers. Emotions buffeted her, tightening her chest and making it hard to catch her breath. Stepping back, she watched as first Sam, and then Nate signed the legal papers that would seal the deal.

Her fingers cramped around the pen Nate passed her. Slick palms and shaking fingers made it difficult to add her signature to theirs. Piper took a deep breath and put pen to paper.

SAM WATCHED Piper place her mark on the contract that

tied them all together. Not the kind of relationship he had in mind, but a start. Her hand paused as the final stroke of ink brushed paper, and it was as though the world held its breath. As she lifted the pen, a rush of air left his lungs, and the tension winding his insides loosened. He didn't normally mix business with pleasure. Then again he'd never been tempted by anyone he'd done business with. Besides, they'd seen her outside of the work environment first.

Weeks of watching her as she sat at the beachfront cafe had slowly boiled his blood until the need to know her in every way possible had slashed his insides like a razor blade. Having an excuse to see her, talk to her, only made his plan easier to execute. Sam would work closely with her to get the new site up and running, all the while he'd woo her—they'd woo her—seduce her until her need matched theirs. By the time she fell into bed with him and Nate, she'd believe it was her idea.

"How soon can you get started?" Sam asked.

She looked up from shuffling papers. "Today, if that suits you both."

"The sooner the better," Nate said.

Sam glanced at his watch. "What about we get some lunch, then get started?"

"That's okay, I'll grab something on the way home and begin working straight away. Should have it done before the day is over."

"Home?"

"Yes. I work from home. I'll just need the access codes and backend information before I go."

"Go?"

Why were her words not making any sense? Sam couldn't get past the fact she intended to leave. She couldn't leave. Not yet. Not ever.

Whoa. Where had that thought come from? Sure, he wanted her in his bed, but *forever*?

"Is there a problem?" Piper asked.

Nate articulated what Sam couldn't. "I think we're just a little confused. You aren't going to work here, in the office?"

"Well, no, I didn't think I would be, but if you'd prefer it that way, I—"

"Yes. We'd prefer you stay here." The words rushed from Sam's mouth.

She took a step back with a wary expression on her face, and he realized he sounded like a lunatic. He dragged in a deep breath and reined himself in. Before he could remove his foot from his mouth and redeem himself, Nate came to the rescue.

"If that would be okay with you, Piper, we'd like you to work here for the initial set up. We're so used to running the whole show ourselves, we're finding it hard to let go of even the smallest part of the business." Nate flashed his lady-killer smile, the one that made women drop their panties, or at least agree to whatever he'd suggested.

"Oh, of course." She visibly relaxed. "I know how it is when you've worked hard to build something from nothing."

Sam breathed easier and finally managed to put his brain and mouth in the same gear. "Sorry." He tried for a sheepish smile, prayed he'd pulled it off. "Until recently, we controlled every aspect of the company, but as we've grown that's proven harder, and it would be stupid to continue working that way."

Piper smiled and Sam felt it all the way down to his toes. The urge to kiss the curve of her plush lips knifed through him. He clenched his fists, his jaw. She turned to gather the rest of her papers, and he closed his eyes and pulled in a lungful of air. Air tinted with the smell of her. Sunshine and vanilla.

The scent brought to mind summer and ice cream. Sam wanted to lick *her* like ice cream. Swipe his tongue along the column of her neck, the slope of her shoulder, the rise of her breast. Blood pounded in his veins, rushed into his cock.

He opened his eyes and turned, angled his body so she wouldn't see the erection straining to break free of the front of his pants. It had only been a few hours since he'd found relief, and still she had him fully erect with just the curl of her mouth, the scent of her skin. Sam needed to either throw her over the table and fuck her senseless or get out of the room. He chose to leave the room.

"I'll go clear some space in the office. Get that information that you need." He strode from the room, but not before taking one last look over his shoulder at the minx who had his insides churning like a vat of molten steel.

3

NATE WATCHED SAM LEAVE. He'd never seen his friend so out of control. Sam had always been the more polished of the two. To see him in such a state of agitation over Piper gave Nate reason to worry, but he didn't have time for that. They needed to get her settled and working on their website. He turned to her and offered a smile.

"Here, I'll take that." He reached for her bag. "Follow me, and we'll have you set up in the office in no time."

He didn't give her time to argue, just headed out of the conference room and across the hall, where Sam had already taken a seat behind his big desk. The T-shaped surface held Sam's workstation and the computer they used to work on their website. Nate motioned with his hand for Piper to take a seat, and he put her bag on the table across from his friend.

"This computer is reserved exclusively for the website. It's state of the art and has all the information you need saved on the hard drive."

She paused in the motion of sitting, suspended midair, and

her head jerked in Nate's direction. "You keep your passwords saved on the computer?"

"Yeah, is that a problem?"

"Of course it is." She sank the rest of the way into the chair he'd pulled out for her. "You should never leave something like that where anyone can access it."

Nate laughed. "Only Sam and I have access to the office. I doubt there's any danger of the passwords getting into the wrong hands."

"But—"

"We have the best alarm system on the market, and as this is also our home, we're extra careful about who we let in here," Sam added.

Piper turned to look at him. "It isn't just those that have direct access to your computer you need to worry about. While I doubt you'd be the target of a hacker you still should be more careful with these things. You should also change your passwords every month."

"Well, now that you'll be looking after that end of the business, you can do whatever you deem necessary to keep us safe." Sam smiled.

"Why don't I go see about lunch while you two get sorted?" Nate offered.

"Um..."

"Great idea, I'm starving. There's lasagna and salad in the fridge—how's that sound to you, Piper?" Sam asked.

"Don't go to any trouble—"

"No trouble at all." Nate placed his hand on her shoulder, felt the heat of her body through the thin layer of cloth. "I've got to fix something for us anyway—one more won't hurt."

He brushed his fingers along her collarbone as he pulled his hand away and could have sworn she shivered under his touch. Nate directed a look at Sam before leaving them to get started, a look that said *don't screw this thing up or I'll pound your ass into the ground.* Confident that his friend got the message, he headed for the stairs to the second floor and the kitchen.

It took him a good thirty minutes to heat the lasagna, but he used the time wisely and set the table. Normally they ate at their desks, but he wanted to bring Piper into the house, wanted to see her in their home, see if she fit like Nate thought she would. He thought about opening a bottle of wine, but nixed that idea. Not for their first lunch together, in the middle of a workday. He'd save the wine for dinner. A smile tugged at his mouth. He had no doubt she'd be staying for dinner.

Nate placed the pan on a hot pad on the table and walked over to the intercom. He pushed the button for the office.

"Lunch is ready."

It took Sam a few seconds to answer, and Nate thought for a split second they'd gotten busy without him, but he soon ruled that out. Sam knew as well as he did that they were in this together. Either they both had Piper or neither of them did, and considering Nate usually got what he wanted, they'd be having her before too much longer.

"On our way."

Nate filled water glasses. He heard them coming up the stairs as he topped off the last one.

"Oh, my gosh, what a gorgeous view." Piper walked over to the glass wall that overlooked the ocean.

"Yeah, it's even better when the doors are open so you can hear the waves hitting the rocks below."

Nate watched her as she stood in front of the window. Her skirt and blouse did nothing for her figure—both were shapeless and gave no clue to the body hidden beneath. But he'd seen her in shorts and mini-skirts over the past few weeks. He knew she had killer legs under that formless black fabric. And the stark white top covered all of her. Why she would wear long sleeves on a day like today escaped him, but the little tank tops she'd worn while sitting in the cafe had given him more than an idea of her ample chest measurements. He couldn't wait to get his hands on her breasts.

~

LUNCH WASN'T AS uncomfortable as Piper thought it would be. They talked about everything from work, to sports, to movies, to favorite authors. She couldn't remember the last time she'd had so much fun with her closest friends, never mind a couple of guys she hardly knew. When they'd eaten the last bite, they continued to talk, and before she knew it nearly two hours had gone by.

"Jeez, look at the time." She stacked dirty plates. "We should clean up and get back to work."

Piper took her pile to the kitchen, separated from the open living-dining area by a long L-shaped counter. On the kitchen side, the island held the sink and prep area, and on the other side, a long counter with six stools formed a breakfast bar. She could imagine sitting there with a morning coffee watching the sunrise over the ocean.

Pip sighed. The water view certainly beat the brick wall she could see through the one poky window in her kitchen. Although the stove, sink, and single cupboard at her place couldn't really be called a kitchen.

Nate and Sam came over with the rest of the dishes, and together they scraped, rinsed, and stacked them in the dish-washer. In no time they had everything put away, wiped down, and the dishwasher humming through the first cycle. Satisfied they'd cleaned up properly, Piper turned to look at the view one more time before getting back to work. It really was the most gorgeous sight. The sun sparkled on the water, and while the mass of blue was calm, there were enough ripples in the surface to make the light dance like diamonds scattered on blue satin.

"That has to be one of the best views in Sydney," she acknowledged.

"We like it. It's one of the reasons we bought the house and renovated it," Sam said.

"It's just as spectacular in winter, especially when a thunderstorm rolls in," Nate added.

Piper could imagine the slashes of lightning, the rolling waves, and the rain pouring down. Yes, she could totally understand the thrill of watching nature's fury as much as the calm beauty before her now. But she had to pull herself away from the window and get back to work. Most of the new site was up, but she hadn't pulled the old down yet, and she wanted to play a bit more with the shopping cart to make sure she'd eliminated any bugs in the purchasing process.

"Enough slacking—your site won't finish itself."

She turned and slammed straight into a wall of hard muscle. Air rushed from her lungs at the impact, warmth surrounded her, enclosed her in a fiery grip that sucked every last atom of oxygen from her body. Strong arms banded around her, and Piper went soft and melted like chocolate on a hot summer day. She leaned in, pressed her breasts against the solid chest, and moaned.

"Piper."

Her name, whispered against her ear, flowed over her. Like warm honey, it coated her skin and sent heat bursting through her veins, teasing every nerve ending. A shiver started in her curled toes and traveled up. Up, up, up, striking at sensitive places with a rush of arousal and need. Desire and want like none she'd known tore open the cage of restraint. She pressed closer, ran her hands over cloth-covered muscles that shuddered beneath her touch. An answering tremor vibrated down her spine.

Hands curled around her ribs, pushed between them, and cupped her breasts as delicious heat covered her back. Piper arched, thrusting her tender mounds and taut nipples into waiting fingers. Lips skimmed her jaw, teeth nipping at her skin. She moved her head to the side at the nudge of a nose and was treated to delicate licks and sucks along the column of her throat.

"So responsive."

"So sweet."

It took a moment for the twin comments murmured against her jaw and neck to register, but when they did, shock bloomed and panic erupted. Piper broke away, jumped from the embrace Nate and Sam held her in. Harsh breaths burned in her chest, scored at her throat, as she stared at the two men before her.

How could she have allowed them to touch her like that? To stand between them as though it were the only place she should be?

"Oh God." Piper brought her hands up to cover her face.

She had no excuse for what she'd done, no explanation. Heat seared her face as embarrassment at her behavior flooded her, doing its best to drown the arousal still swimming in her blood. But nothing short of a tidal wave could douse the flames blazing inside her core. Pip spun on her heel, ready to bolt for the door, but she hadn't taken two steps when she found herself once again caught between two hot male bodies.

Gasping and trembling, she buried her face against Nate's soft cotton shirt and prayed for the ground to open up and swallow her whole. Why was there never a good sinkhole when you needed one? And why think about stupid holes in the ground when she was trapped between two of the most gorgeous men she'd ever met? Had she gone mad?

With a sigh, Piper realized she should pull away, but thinking and doing were two different things, and arguing with herself about doing it didn't help. Her body wanted to stay right there, but her brain that kept screaming this is wrong had her trying to tug from their embrace.

"Please, let me go."

~

"ON ONE CONDITION. NO RUNNING." Nate wasn't about to let her go completely. She'd been with them in the beginning, but something spooked her and she'd bolted. Now they just had to identify the problem and make it go away.

He held still, waited for her to answer, and hoped to hell he wouldn't need to tie her to a chair to keep her here. There were more interesting places to tie her up if it came to that. Nate chanced a quick glance at Sam. They'd sandwiched her between them, each gripping a handful of the other's shirt, effectively caging her with their arms.

When she mumbled against his chest, he felt her lips move and her breath burned through his shirt to his skin. The heat shot fire through his veins and hardened his cock further. She couldn't miss the erection pressing into her belly.

"What did you say?" Sam asked.

Piper raised her head enough to make the words audible. "Okay."

His gaze connected with Sam's. Together they released their grip and stepped back. She stood with her head down, and her chest rose and fell with the labored breaths she dragged in. Nate wanted to reach out and soothe her, tell her everything would be all right, but he knew if he touched her again, he'd not be letting go until he'd buried himself inside her a dozen times and slaked the savage lust riding his backbone.

"Why don't we go into the lounge and sit down?" Nate didn't wait for either of them to agree. He turned and headed over to his recliner, figuring he'd keep his distance. For now.

When he turned to sit in his chair, he saw Sam had followed him. Piper still stood near the window, a good thirty feet away, but she hadn't run yet, so that was a start. He got comfortable and waited. His patience would only go so far, but he knew in his gut he needed to pull on that virtue for all he was worth. He felt as though the woman across the room held his future happiness in her hands. The fact she didn't have a clue gave him mild relief, but everything rode on the next few minutes.

He watched her closely, concentrated on the small movements of her body. Her breathing eased and the hands at her sides unclenched. Those breasts he so wanted to get his hands on rose with a deep, indrawn breath. Then she lifted her head, and shoulders back, walked in their direction.

She perched her cute ass on the very edge of the couch, poised for a quick getaway, no doubt. But there wouldn't be one. Nate had no intention of letting her get away from them. Not after she'd gone pliant in his arms.

"Let's lay it out on the table, no games." Nate looked at Sam. "We've watched you for weeks."

Piper's gaze snapped to his, big brown eyes wide in shock and her plush, pink lips parted.

"Yeah, we've seen you. This morning we decided to approach you tomorrow, except here you are on our doorstep today."

"Best thing I ever opened the door for." Sam said. "And then, when you fell into my arms...well, who could ask for more?"

Nate kept a close eye on her. Observed all the telltale signs her body gave off. If he wasn't mistaken, Sam's words pleased her.

"I don't know what to say."

"Then don't say anything until we're finished. Just listen." At her nod, Nate continued. "We want you."

She sucked in a breath and those lovely breasts thrust forward. He couldn't miss the hard nipples pushing against her blouse.

"Together," Sam added.

Her breathing hitched and she squirmed in her seat. With her gaze darting from one to the other, Nate decided to up the ante.

"We want you in our bed, Piper. We've wanted you for weeks. Neither of us has touched another woman since laying eyes on you."

"You got under our skin long before we knew your name." Sam moved forward in his chair. "We want to see where this could go."

"But..."

Nate leaned forward in his seat. "Don't deny you feel it, Piper. This thing between us has sizzled in the room all morning."

When she pushed to her feet, Nate and Sam instantly came to theirs. Stepped closer. They left nowhere for her to go; the couch rested at the back of her legs and they stood in front of her.

"I didn't—"

Nate placed a finger over her lips. "Don't lie, Piper." Moist air bathed his skin. "Don't do that to us, or yourself."

"We know you feel it too." Sam brushed his fingers along her cheek, up around her ear, and down along her jaw. She shivered.

"I don't—"

He trailed his finger back and forth over her bottom lip. "Yes, you do." His fingertips caressed her feathery eyelashes. "It's in the way your eyes go as dark as night." Nate brought his hand down along her nose. "It's in the hitch of your breath." Pressing his fingers to the pulse beating in the hollow of her throat, he said, "It's in the pounding of your heart." He grazed his nails lower, into the shadowy depths of her cleavage. "And it's in the quiver running beneath your skin when we touch you."

A shudder rippled through her and she leaned into their caresses. Sam cupped her right breast as Nate weighed her left one in the palm of his hand. Her breath caught in her chest and the tight nipple drew up bullet-hard against his flesh. Nate smiled. He found her the most responsive woman he'd ever had the pleasure of touching, and he planned to do plenty of touching during their seduction of Piper.

4

SAM'S HAND trembled as he held Piper's supple flesh. The warm, rounded underslope of her breast sat snug in his palm as if they'd been made for each other. He pinched the protruding nipple with thumb and forefinger, tweaked and twisted until the bud grew hard as granite and a whimper tripped off her tongue. The need to taste her sliced into him. First he'd sample her mouth and then every other inch of her luscious body. With deliberate slowness, he eased forward, brought their lips together in the barest of touches.

From the corner of his eye, he saw Nate drop his head to her left breast. The second his friend's lips wrapped around her shirt-covered nipple, she gasped, and Sam dove deep. He stabbed his tongue between her parted lips and invaded her mouth. Moist heat laced with spice greeted him. Dark recesses had no defense against his assault. Sam stroked and nipped, teasing them both until urgency took hold, dragged them deeper into the carnal delight of their kiss.

Piper gave and took in equal measure. Her tongue tangled with his; her teeth scraped and those plump lips widened to draw him further in. He was lost. She surrounded him, filled him, pulled him in with moans and gasps. Sam felt Nate's mouth next to his; moving aside slightly, he let his friend in. Three mouths meshed, three tongues dueled. For seconds he let himself slide down the slippery slope into bliss before it was snatched out from under him.

She pulled herself from their embrace. Panting for breath, Piper climbed over the couch and away from them.

"What the hell?" Nate moved toward her, but she scrambled out of reach, putting the large piece of furniture between them.

Sam stilled his friend with a hand on his shoulder. Putting the brakes on the lust ripping through his body proved difficult, but he knew he had to take a step back or Piper would run out the door, not just to the other side of the room. For long moments, the three of them stared at each other, the combined rasp of their fractured breaths the only sound in the room. With a small measure of fear, Sam stepped back and took his seat once more. Nate followed his lead, and he hoped their retreat would allow her to relax enough to talk to them. He'd known this would be a tricky situation to begin with, and after what had just happened, they would need to tread lightly.

Sam watched Piper. Her breathing and the trembling fingers covering her mouth told him she was just as stirred up as they were. Would she do something about it or walk away?

She eyed them both for a considerable amount of time, minutes that dragged over his nerves like a rusty nail. Finally, she moved around the couch to perch on the edge of the leather seat, ready to bolt at any moment.

"You kissed me." The words were muffled behind her hand.

"Yes, we did," Sam agreed.

"You both kissed me."

He couldn't help himself; he grinned. "Yes, we certainly did."

"Together." Her voice wobbled, whether from excitement, fear, or disgust he aimed to find out.

"We told you we both wanted you," Nate added.

Piper nodded. "But you kissed each other."

The astonishment in her words couldn't be missed, but Sam thought she appeared shocked by their actions, not disgusted. He glanced at Nate, and at his nod, took the lead on explaining their complex relationship.

"We don't do it often—"

"You're *gay?*"

Nate let out a snort, and Sam couldn't hold back his own chuckle. "Piper, we had our hands on you, our mouths on you. Christ, our tongues were down your throat, and we've both got boners we could use for hammers. Does that sound like we're gay?"

"But...but...you kissed each other."

"We've done more than kiss," Nate murmured, and Sam silenced him with a look. *One step at a time.*

"We were kissing you. Together. We thought we were giving you pleasure. I know you liked it before your brain decided to throw up a road block."

She nodded but didn't speak.

He took a deep breath. "Nate and I sometimes share the woman we're seeing, although not always, and we've never both wanted the same woman to the degree we want you."

"I got that part, but you kissed each other."

"While kissing you, Piper." Nate fidgeted in the seat and Sam recognized his friends growing frustration.

"Look, it's hard to explain the dynamics of our relationship. We're best mates, have been for years, and at some point we stepped over a line into a deeper connection, first by sharing a woman and then by being with each other. But we're not satisfied with just each other; that's not all we need, and what we have isn't like what we have with a woman." Sam shook his head. "I'm not making this very clear."

"What Sam and I share is rougher, more driven than what we'd share with you. It allows all the parts of our personalities to be satisfied. I don't think you can fully understand it without experiencing it."

Piper looked at Nate. "So you're not gay. Bisexual then?"

Sam laughed. "Nope, no desire to be with any other guy but him." He hooked his thumb in Nate's direction. "Do we have to label what we are?"

She looked down at her hands. They were twisting in her lap, her knuckles turning white. "No, I guess not, but it's a habit I have. I like to put things in the right place, and you can't do that without knowing what it is to begin with."

"Okay, so put this in the pleasure box." Nate leaned forward. "Label it pleasure and just enjoy it."

"Enjoy it?"

"Yes. Enjoy it with us." Sam indicated both of them. "Let us show you how good it can be. You don't have to do anything that makes you uncomfortable, we won't push you or make you do anything you don't want to, and it'll all be about pleasure."

"I don't know." She wrung her hands tighter. "I've never done anything..."

When she didn't continue, Sam had a horrible thought, but before he could voice it, Nate almost fell out of his chair.

"You're a virgin?"

⌒

"WHAT? NO!" Pip stared at Nate; heat flared in her cheeks and she quickly ducked her head again.

"Then what did you mean, 'you've never done anything?'" Sam asked.

Her face flamed hotter. "I've had sex." She swallowed over her dry throat and mumbled, "Just not much of it."

Living her whole life in the same small town with three older brothers didn't exactly lend itself to freedom of any kind. It was hard enough to date without everyone knowing about it, never mind actually having sex with a date.

"How old are you, Piper? Twenty-one, twenty-two?"

Piper's head snapped up, her gaze locked on Sam's. "Twenty-seven. Twenty-eight next month." Her hackles rose at his skeptical look. "I can show you my driver's license if you want proof."

"No, that's okay, I believe you. But to be honest I thought twenty-one was pushing it. I'd started to feel like a dirty old man." He laughed.

She understood where he came from. Looking years younger than her age had always been a pain in the ass. Depending on what she wore, she still looked like a teenager, so her family treated her like one. She'd moved to Sydney to get away from the people who spent way too much time smothering her for her own good. The move had been about making her own choices and experiencing life how she wanted to, not how someone else said she should want to.

"So how many times have you had sex?" Nate asked. He'd been quiet since his last question.

"Umm…" Piper didn't want these two sexy men knowing how few times she'd had sex. Crap, they'd definitely change their mind about wanting her if they knew, and she wasn't about to let this opportunity pass her by. Two hot, gorgeous men wanted her in their bed. She could only imagine the things they could show her—do to her, *with* her. Moisture soaked her panties as her pussy clenched. She wasn't a complete stranger to pleasure. Granted, most of what she knew she'd learned on her own, but still, she'd had orgasms.

Sam rescued her. "Maybe an exact number isn't necessary. The question is, are you interested in having sex with us? Together?"

Both men watched her closely. She tried not to squirm but found it hard with her body on fire from the wicked images that had sprung to mind. With the sensations of their earlier attention still fresh, Piper wanted to rip off her clothes and throw herself on the floor in front of them. But a good amount of fear thrummed through her alongside the arousal, and she didn't think jumping into this with both feet would be the right thing for any of them. There were other factors. For a start, they'd just signed a contract that would keep them in contact for the next twelve months. If something went wrong...

Piper had a lot to lose if things got messy, and sex always complicated everything. Damn. She really wanted to take what they offered. If she lived to be a hundred, she'd never get another opportunity like this one. With the small taste of what they could make her feel still vibrating across her nerves, she struggled to remain sensible. It would be so easy to fall into them and to hell with the consequences, but Piper had never been one to leap into anything without weighing all the possibilities.

"Your body tells us you want to say yes, Piper, but I think your mind is doing its best to stop you."

She looked at Sam. He was right, of course. Her body screamed to accept, and honesty forced her to admit her mind was half convinced as well, but there still remained that one thing...

"This has no bearing on our contract," Nate said. "Regardless of whether you say yes, the agreement is still binding, and we won't hold it against you if you decline to sleep with us."

Jeez, could they read her mind?

"And that goes the other way too. No repercussions if you say yes, either," Sam added.

"No strings at all," Nate finished.

Piper chewed the inside of her cheek to stop the word yes from leaving her mouth. Could there be no strings? Could she go ahead and enjoy these two sexy men, *her boys*, without worry? They were older than her by at least five years and had an existing relationship—she'd also be the third wheel most of the time. If she looked at this as just sex, just the mutual giving and taking of pleasure and nothing more, then it would be unlikely she'd develop any real feelings toward them.

Piper had experienced sex four times in her life, with four different guys, none of whom she'd been in love with, and after the act, she certainly hadn't felt any more tender feelings. She believed she could sleep with Sam and Nate without becoming emotionally involved. They'd said they would honor the contract, and Pip was one hundred percent sure they would. For some reason, she trusted them. Their home and business showed their dedication and reliability, and a gut-deep knowledge inside her agreed it would be fine to place herself in their capable hands.

Lord knew if it was her hormones talking or not, but Piper had always been a good judge of character. Her intuition had never steered her wrong before.

Besides, if she agreed and went into this with her eyes wide open, then she'd see what was coming before it hit her, wouldn't she? And if she saw the danger, she could remove herself from the situation and not get hurt. And if she said no, she'd miss out on experiencing what promised to be the greatest pleasure of her life.

"There's no rush, Piper." Sam stood up. "Why don't we

finish putting the new site in place and then the three of us can have dinner together. See where things go?"

"Good idea. We've got to head over to the Baker Street site to check on a few things this afternoon, so you'll have the office all to yourself for a few hours." Nate pushed out of his chair and came to stand in front of her. "No pressure, Piper, and we'll respect whatever decision you make."

Piper watched as he turned and walked away. Her eyes were drawn to his ass, the way his pants stretched taut across one of the best butts she'd had the pleasure of admiring. When Nate was out of sight, she dragged her attention back to Sam who still stood in front of her. The knowing smile on his face brought heat to her cheeks again, but she refused to hide it this time.

"He has one of the most gorgeous asses I've ever seen," she said.

Sam laughed. "Can't argue with you there, but you might want to take a peek in the mirror at your own behind. That's some world class buttage right there."

His words made her blush more and when she got to her feet her knees shook. "Well, guess I should get back to work."

Gesturing with his arm, Sam said, "Lead the way."

Heat crawled up her spine. She could feel Sam's eyes on her, his gaze a hot heavy weight that sent sparks of arousal shooting into her core, pulling more moisture from deep inside. Piper's feminine wiles had her putting a little extra swing in her step; behind her Sam stifled a groan.

They made their way down the spiral staircase, the open steps and wrought iron balustrade giving an airy feeling to the floors it served. From what Pip could see it went up one more level from the kitchen lounge area, and then down to the ground floor where the office she'd been working in was located. The stairs continued below street height to what she assumed was the basement. Sun streamed through the round holes the stairs made in each story, splashing out bright golden sunbeams to illuminate the house and stop it from being dark and dreary.

The office ran along both sides of the building and across the back with the foyer, front doors, and staircase taking up the rest of the space. Other than the conference room, the workspace was open and spacious with the back wall being all glass like the upstairs. The exception being these windows were covered with timber shutters angled to let in light but block enough so the glare wasn't too bright to work. Piper returned to the desk she'd used earlier and pulled the chair out. She hadn't forgotten Sam behind her, but she still jumped when he reached around her to grab the chair like they were about to sit down in a fancy restaurant.

"Thank you." Piper slipped into the seat, careful not to brush up against him in any way. It didn't matter that they'd shelved the sex for later. Her body still hummed with arousal and her mind kept rolling that mental filmstrip of images, each one more scandalous than the last. She licked her lips, her parched mouth and throat making it difficult to swallow.

"You're welcome." Sam removed his hand from the chair. His fingers brushed the top of her shoulder and trailed up to graze the delicate skin of her neck. A shiver wracked her, each tiny vibration leaving goose bumps behind.

She closed her eyes, struggled to hold back the moan in her throat. He stepped away, the loss of heat against her back noticeable. Piper waited, for what she didn't know, but the very room seemed to hold its breath as her body fought the onslaught of desire that saturated every nerve ending.

Drowning in her own lust, she barely heard Sam speak. Barely saw the piece of paper he placed in front of her with both his and Nate's phone numbers on it. When he finally left the room, all the air that had backed up in her lungs exploded in a gust of desperation.

With a groan, Pip wondered how she would make it through the afternoon without dying. She burned with an ache foreign to all she'd known, an ache that threatened to be her undoing. But with the ragged edge of desire came the slice of pleasure, and with every soothing breath she drew into her lungs, she knew she'd never be the same again, never know the sweet innocence in which she'd lived before now.

The thumping beat of her heart became a timekeeper to the last seconds of an existence that would soon experience untold ecstasy. A sliver of fear stabbed her. Could she go through with it? She had to.

Because once her *Bondi Beach Boys* returned, there'd be no going back.

5

NATE TURNED his wrist and glanced at his watch for the hundredth time since arriving at the job site.

"Stop it. Time isn't going to go quicker just because you're staring at it." Sam growled in frustration.

Nate eyed his mate, took in the taut muscles and frown lines in his forehead. "Like you're not wishing the day was over any less than I am."

"Never said I wasn't, but with you looking at that fucking watch every second, you're driving both of us fucking insane."

The tight line of muscles along Nate's back loosened. Just by knowing he wasn't alone in his torture brought relief. But it couldn't reduce the fear. "What if she says no?"

Sam shrugged and gave him that know-it-all grin. "Not much we can do except pull out every dirty trick we know to convince her to say yes."

"Seduce her?"

"Hell yeah! You tasted her. Can you honestly walk away without having more?"

Damn. Sam was right. That one little sample only whetted his appetite for more. "So what's the plan?"

"Don't bring it up."

Nate cocked an eyebrow and looked at Sam dubiously.

"We go home, ask about the site upload, get her to demonstrate. By then dinner will arrive because we'll order that before we get home. She's less likely to say no to the meal if it's there in front of her and smelling delicious."

Nate nodded. So far Sam's plan sounded good.

"I'll open a bottle of wine to have with dinner. We'll keep the conversation light and easy, keep the mood mellow. Three people enjoying a meal and each other's company. Then one of us can suggest a movie. You'll make popcorn, and we'll drink more wine."

"Damn you're good." Nate shook his head. "Sometimes the way your mind works scares me. I'm seduced just by listening."

Sam's smile spread. "Yeah, but you're easy."

Nate rolled his eyes. "Jeez, don't go telling everyone." He glanced around but no one else was in this bedroom of the two-story refurb they were currently doing. Good thing too because he couldn't hide the boner currently tenting the front of his pants.

"Wanna shut the door and deal with that?"

He looked back at Sam who eyed his groin with interest. Nate thought about it, thought it wasn't a bad idea, breaking the hard ridge of need currently consuming him, but he doubted it would soothe him for long. Nothing short of having Piper under him, over him, around him, and trapped between him and Sam would bring relief now.

Nate palmed his cock. Squeezed the throbbing flesh confined under his zipper. "Now that the taste of Piper is coating my tongue, there'll be no dealing with this unless she's involved."

Sam sighed. "I know. The only thing that has a hope in hell of appeasing me at the moment is holding her between us."

Nate could picture it. Could imagine her soft ass snug against his hips, his chest pressed along her spine, and the feel of her skin as it molded to his. He could see Sam as he flattened his front to hers, her breasts crushed by the hard wall of his chest. She'd wither, rock her hips, and drive them all insane until they moaned and searched for bliss in each other.

"Fuck!" Sam gave him a shove. "Stop. Whatever the fuck you were thinking, stop!" He paced two steps away, spun and came back, got right into Nate's face. "Jesus. I have no idea what just went through your head, but I can imagine well enough. If you want to push us both over the edge, keep going, but if you don't rein it in you're going to scare the shit out of Piper. You do that, and I'll ground you into dust."

Nate stared into Sam's eyes, saw the raw hunger, the naked fear behind his words, and swallowed. Until this moment, he hadn't really believed they were in the same place where Piper was concerned. He'd thought the insane emotions boiling inside him were his and his alone. Sure, he knew they both wanted her physically, that was a given, but after spending the morning and lunch with her...

"How can she mean so much? We don't even really know her."

Sam closed his eyes, dragged in a deep breath, and ran a hand over his face. "I don't know man, but she does." His friend's shoulders sagged a little.

"We can't fuck this up," Nate said.

"No. We can't."

SAM PULLED the pickup into the underground garage and

shut off the engine. Neither of them got out. They sat there in the quiet, each caught in his own thoughts for several minutes. He blew out a breath and reached for the door handle.

"Let's get started."

"Right behind you." Nate jumped out the other side and slammed the door. He walked around and met Sam at the door to the basement. "Do you think we ordered the right food? What if she doesn't like Chinese?"

He wanted to laugh at Nate's obsessing, but he couldn't. It matched the streak of fear running down his spine that his best mate might be right. "Everyone loves Chinese," he said with a hint of desperation lacing the words.

"Yeah, you're right. It'll be fine."

The air around them seemed to vibrate with their anxiety. How one woman could reduce them both to scared little boys in less than a day Sam didn't have a clue, but that's exactly what Piper had done. They made their way up the stairs. He could hear Piper muttering in the office as they neared the door. Two feet inside the room they came to a complete standstill. There in front of them on her hands and knees was Piper. Her delectable ass wiggling as she backed out from under the desk. Sam sucked in a breath as every muscle in his body tensed.

Blood rushed past his ears as it left his brain for areas further south. His cock thickened, lengthened, filling the space behind his zipper and threatening to do some damage if he didn't do some rearranging soon. Next to him, Nate groaned and the raw sound of need dragged across Sam's skin like nails on a chalkboard, sent a fist sized knot into his gut, and dropped tingling weight into his balls. Sam made a strangled sound that brought Piper upright, but she hadn't cleared the desk and the back of her head smacked against the timber edge.

Her cry of pain had them both charging across the room.

On their knees beside her in less than a second, Nate pulled her into his arms and Sam rubbed the bump forming on her skull. Piper looked up at him and if he hadn't been on his knees already the tears in her eyes would have taken him there.

"You need an ice pack. Some pain pills." Sam started to stand but Piper placed her hand on his arm to stop.

"No. I'm okay." She smiled but he wasn't reassured. "It's just a little bump, not much more than a sting."

He wasn't convinced but when she pulled from Nate's embrace and stood up on steady legs, he decided a trip to the hospital wouldn't be necessary. The thought brought him up short. Since when was he prone to panic? He worked in construction and restoration, and never in all the years of workplace accidents had he ever felt the bone-shaking terror he did now. And over a little bump on the head? Sam glanced at Nate and saw the same concern and fear in his eyes. The sight made him feel marginally better, but only because he wasn't making a complete fool of himself on his own.

"Are you sure you don't need an ice pack?" Nate asked as he got to his feet to stand beside Piper.

"No, the sting is almost gone now." She ran her hand over the lump on the back of her head. "See? It's not even tender to touch."

Sam got up and stretched to his full height. He looked down at Piper and examined her eyes. They didn't appear glassy any longer and the pupils seemed normal, but then he wasn't a doctor, so what would he know. The doorbell sounded, interrupting his thoughts and his probing stare.

"That'll be dinner." He wrapped his fingers around her arm, cupped her elbow in his palm, and began to steer her toward the door.

"Dinner?"

"Yes. We ordered Chinese on the way home."

"But—"

"Don't argue. You've just had a bump on the head, and you need to rest." Sam strode to the stairs while Nate went to collect their food and pay the delivery guy. "You can eat while you rest."

"Sam, that's not necessary. If you'll just let me finish up work for the day, I'll call a taxi and head home."

"No."

The one word, said with a hint of steel in his voice, stilled her protests and allowed him to continue on up to the living room.

He nudged her onto the couch and said, "Don't move. I'll get some plates and forks."

Drawers slammed and cupboard doors banged as he took his frustration out on the kitchen. Sam fought with the swirling emotions Piper provoked without much effort and wondered what the hell was happening to him. Nate walked in and dropped the bags on the granite counter. Quickly, they pulled out the plastic food containers and filled three plates. Sam placed the leftovers in the oven and picked up his plate and the utensils while Nate grabbed his and Piper's dinner and headed for the lounge.

They were almost finished eating when Sam realized he'd forgotten to open the wine. There'd been no conversation over dinner, but the silence wasn't uncomfortable in any way. In fact it had been rather pleasant, the three of them consuming their meals as the last of the summer light faded outside. As far as the seduction plan went, tonight had turned out to be a bust. He leaned forward, put his empty plate on the coffee table in front of them, and then relaxed back into his seat.

Piper's scent combined with the smell of Chinese food made a strange erotic concoction that tantalized his senses. Sam watched as she picked up a king prawn and popped it into her mouth. The sauce coated her lips and glistened in the twilight, her jaw moved as she chewed the succulent morsel, and he wanted to nibble on her. His gaze remained glued to her when she swallowed, the smooth column of her throat flexing as the muscles worked, and he wondered if it would look the same if she were swallowing his come.

THE BUMP on her head didn't hurt as much as the ache in her core. From the second Piper had sensed them behind her in the office, her body had twisted into a coil of need that made her blood heat and pump through her veins like lava. Her breathing came in choppy bursts, the effort to fill her lungs almost too difficult to manage. She felt hot and swollen all over and her clothes itched her skin like a thousand unseen prickles. How she'd made it through dinner without melting into the couch was anyone's guess.

She put her plate, still loaded with food, on top of Sam's. They'd sat on either side of her, their body heat doing nothing to help her gain control of her rampaging hormones.

How did these two men drive her to distraction without trying?

What was it about them that pulled unknown needs and wants from deep inside her?

Needs and wants Piper had had no clue existed until they'd yanked them from her.

Urges and desires so outside her universe she could be on an alien planet.

Piper leaned back against the soft leather seat. Sam's hand brushed the back of her neck where it rested stretched along the top of the lounge. Shivers rippled over her, taking delicious waves of sensation to sensitive flesh already plump with arousal. Her nipples hardened, the two buds drawing up tight as desire laced intricate patterns between her breasts and pussy. Inner walls clenched, sending hot cream into her undies. His fingertips toyed with her hair and more shudders rolled over her.

Nate finished his meal and added his plate to the bottom of the pile. It took all her concentration to watch the mundane action and not whimper with need. She must have made a sound though because Nate's head jerked around and his gaze collided with hers.

Banked flames burst to life in the dark brown depths, and Piper's breath stalled in her lungs. He stared at her with such naked longing that her core pulsed, her clit throbbed. Sam's fingers cupped her neck and tugged her face around to his.

"Piper?"

Her name held the question on both their minds and fell from his lips as barely a whisper. Each letter tripped across her nerve endings to tangle with the yearning that grew stronger with every breath. Sam's eyes burned with a hunger to match Nate's. To match hers. Moisture soaked her panties, coated her flesh and filled the air around them with the scent of desire. All thought fled and only one word echoed in her head. *Yes.*

"*Yes.*" She slurred the word and moaned, her lungs and throat unable to function properly.

Twin growls dropped harshly over her before Sam took her mouth with his. His tongue thrust deep, penetrating her with little finesse, but her body didn't seem to mind the roughness. Her breasts grew heavy, and when hands cupped the tender globes, she didn't care who they belonged to. Sam continued to lay claim to her mouth, and she surrendered beneath the onslaught. Spirals of heat wound their way through her. Fabric ripped and buttons popped as their hands worked to free her of the restriction.

Not to be outdone, Piper's hands sought to push aside cloth until her fingers encountered warm male flesh. She gasped as heat seared her skin. Her nails raked over hard muscle, and Nate's groan told her who she touched. Sam pulled his mouth from hers, leaving both of them panting for breath. Piper struggled to raise her heavy eyelids and couldn't remember when she'd closed them. They both tugged their shirts off over their head, tossing them to the floor. Next they removed the tattered remains of her blouse, the garment ruined in their haste to undress her.

"God, you're gorgeous." Nate traced a finger along the lace edge of her bra, the gentle caress a contradiction to the frantic needs of moments before.

"I want you naked on a bed. Stretched out so I can look at you, touch every part of you." Sam's words drew tantalizing images in her head.

"Yes."

Her whispered agreement had both men moving quickly. Piper found herself cradled in Sam's arms as he followed Nate to the stairs. They ascended them two at a time, and she marveled at the effortless way Sam carried her to the bed he'd spoken of. There was no time to take in the room they entered. Sam lowered her to her feet and while he held her in the cradle of his arms, Nate went to work on her skirt. In no time she stood in the glow of moonlight in nothing more than two strips of lace.

"Jesus Christ, you're wearing a G-string."

Nate's strangled words had Sam pushing her to arm's length and spinning her around.

"Fuck." Sam's curse stabbed into the room, into her core.

The thin strap between her legs quickly became saturated with her essence, the scent wafting up to her nostrils. Embarrassed by how wet she was, Piper curled in on herself, and wrapped her arms around her middle.

"Don't." Nate gripped her wrist, pulled them out and away from her body. "You're the most gorgeous thing I've ever seen."

Sam's fingers trailed over the slope of her ass and she started at the hot contact on her bare skin. "You have a beautiful ass." He palmed each cheek. "Firm but soft. It's going to feel fantastic against my hips when I drive my cock between these sweet cheeks and fuck your tight hole."

Her ass clenched and unclenched, Sam's dark promise something she never expected to want, but she couldn't deny the ache his words brought. Piper's hips bucked, driving her bottom back into his hands. He squeezed her hard, pulled and pushed her quivering behind. A moan slipped from her throat, and Nate caught it with his lips. His mouth took hers, his tongue stoking and caressing until she melted into him. Sam continued to ply her backside, his actions driving the thin material of her undies between her pussy lips. The strip of cloth rode her clit, rubbed and pressed, sparking the first waves of her orgasm.

Piper felt her body clench then explode like molten steel. Spasm after spasm rocked her. Sam's teeth nipped her shoulder, and Nate's bit at her jaw. Tongues licked out to soothe and she jerked with the final waves of her release. Cream gushed from her core, and slid down her thighs in a hot bath of satisfaction. She sagged, Nate and Sam the only things stopping her from dissolving on the floor at their feet.

6

SAM HELD Piper's hips as they bucked with her orgasm. She'd gone off like a firecracker, one of those short-fused ones. Her sensitive body responded to everything, from the lightest brush of his fingertips to the press of his palm. The unexpected release tore through her, and he and Nate could only hold on. His cock strained in his pants. Blood pounded a hard beat he couldn't ignore. He wanted to bury himself in her tight body, wanted to feel her soft flesh clutching at him as she came.

She slumped between them, their grip keeping her from collapsing to the floor. Sam looked at Nate, saw his hunger to have her staring back. He tilted his head, indicated the bed, and together they lifted her off her feet and carried her the short distance. Nate reached down and ripped the covers off, tossing them to the floor at the foot of the bed. They lowered Piper to the crisp black sheet that remained. Spent from her orgasm, she flopped to the mattress like a rag doll.

Her hair fanned out around her head, her arms and legs splayed to the side. The white lace bra and underwear she wore were a stark contrast to the rosy-pink flush staining her skin and the dark sheet beneath her. Slumberous eyes looked at them from under lowered lids. Her dark lashes fluttered, and her tongue darted out to wet her bottom lip. Sam's groan echoed Nate's. He reached down to rid himself of his pants. Nate mimicked his actions, and soon they were clothed only in boxer briefs and crawling up the bed on either side of her.

Sam used one hand to flick the clasp between her breasts undone. She wasn't large but ample enough to satisfy him. He palmed one curve, the nipple puckering at his touch. With finger and thumb he pinched the taut peak, plucked and twisted until she writhed beneath him. Her sensitivity blew him away and he tugged harder, wanting to deliver a sharp burst of pleasure-pain before leaning down to lave the tormented tip with his tongue. Piper's flavor and scent filled him, stole inside until it touched him gut deep.

Nate locked his lips to Piper's and Sam watched their tongues tangle in a slow sensuous slide. His sac tightened, his balls tucking up against his groin. Fire lanced his cock, and pre-come leaked from the tip. He trailed his teeth over her flesh, down her ribs, and across her belly. She sucked in a breath, and Sam zeroed in on the indent of her bellybutton. Teasing the dip with his tongue, he took his time enjoying the smooth skin and sweet taste of her. Her stomach quivered under his ministrations, the slight flutter tickling his lips.

The scent of her cream surrounded him, the rich aroma more potent this close to her pussy. Sam wanted to lick up every drop until she screamed with another release. Moving lower, he angled toward her hipbone. Nibbling the sharp ridge, he followed the line until he buried his nose in the hollow where hip met thigh and the soaking wet cloth of her G-string. Her taste exploded on his tongue; her scent coated his nostrils and filled his lungs. Curling his fingers under the lacy material in his way, Sam shifted it aside and stared at the dark hair and plump pink lips.

Oh God!

She'd killed him. There could be no other explanation for the maelstrom of emotions colliding inside him. He'd died and gone to heaven. He breathed deep, drew in all that spicy-sweet perfume that was uniquely hers and savored it. Blowing a burst of hot air over her exposed pussy, he held her thighs to the bed as she jolted. Sam couldn't hold back any more; he had to taste all of her. Sitting up, he gripped the narrow crotch of her undies and ripped it apart. He tossed the triangle covering her mound back to land on her stomach, and the string disappearing into the crack of her ass fell to the bed.

Sam raised her leg and slipped beneath it to rest on his knees between her spread thighs. He grabbed her ankles and pushed them up and back toward her chest. Nate's hands wrapped around her knees, spreading her wider, and the view Sam now had stole his breath. Saliva pooled in his mouth and he leaned down to take his first taste. Swiping his tongue over her clit, he watched her face. Her eyes closed and her head thrashed on the bed. Hands splayed on either side of her cunt as he held her open and began to feast.

Sexy little moans filled the air as he used his tongue to tease her higher. He flicked at her clit, probed at her opening, and tongued the pucker skin lower down, never staying in one place for too long so she wouldn't come before he wanted her to. Over and over he pushed her to the edge, only to pull her back again. At one point he glanced up to see that Nate had his cock free of his pants and was feeding it to Piper, his shaft wet with her saliva, sliding in and out of her red lips. Doubling his efforts, Sam dove back between the slick folds of her cunt.

He licked, nibbled, and sucked. Every dip, every curve, every channel. No part of her went undiscovered. Sam laved from bottom to top and back again. Probed and stroked, drove her toward the peak with single-minded determination to watch her shatter again. She shuddered beneath him, the first waves of her orgasm clenching the walls of her pussy as he thrust as deep as he could inside her with his pointed tongue. Retreating, he swept up to her clit, sucked the bundle of nerves between his lips, and clamped his teeth around the protruding nub.

Piper moaned and her hips bucked, driving her mound into his mouth. She made slurping sounds as she sucked Nate's cock and Sam thought he would lose it. He wanted inside her, needed to ram her cunt with the burning shaft trapped against his stomach. Sam glanced up and saw that Nate had dropped a handful of condoms on the bed near her hip. Letting go of her with one hand, he reached for the nearest one. Panic filled him when he realized he'd have to stop eating her out to open the foil packet. The groan that left his throat vibrated on her clit, and she jerked under him, the motion forcing him to let go.

She whimpered around Nate's erection, the sound a protest and needy cry rolled into one. Sam used his teeth to tear the wrapper and remove the protection, but the extra lubrication made for a slippery juggling act with only one hand. The fingers of his other hand parted her folds and he leaned in to lick at her again. Cream flowed from her, coating her pussy and thighs, his chin. Tormenting her with his tongue, Sam managed to shove his boxers down and sheath his throbbing cock. Nate still held one of her knees so Sam had little trouble accessing all of her.

Sam drove two fingers into her pussy, thrust hard, and sucked her clit between his teeth. She screamed around Nate's cock and exploded under his mouth. Cream gushed over his fingers and hand, and her hips thrashed on the bed but he didn't let up. He dropped his thumb and pressed on the tight ring of muscle guarding her ass. A second orgasm swamped the first and her cunt squeezed his fingers. Her anus clenched and unclenched, allowing his thumb to sink knuckle deep.

"Yes. That's it, Piper, come for us. Suck my cock harder. Deeper."

Nate's words snapped Sam to attention and he pulled away from her body's greedy grip. He quickly raised her pelvis from the bed and lined the head of his cock up to her grasping pussy. In one hard, fast thrust, he sank balls-deep in her quivering hole. Sam held her legs against his chest as he pounded into her. Nate moved, his hands now buried in her hair, holding her still while he fucked her mouth. Saliva glistened along his friend's shaft, coated her lips, and dribbled down her chin.

He watched, mesmerized by the sight of his best mate taking her hard and fast while he strained for release. Sam's own orgasm boiled in his groin, bubbled out to spread over his balls and cock, push up his spine in a tingling trail that warned of the imminent explosion. The final contractions of her muscles rippled over his length and pulled the pin.

Like a grenade, he detonated with a ferocity that robbed him of breath and blew him away.

NATE WATCHED Sam lose himself in Piper's body and knew he followed right behind him. His balls burned with the need to come but he wasn't sure if she wanted to swallow or not. He didn't want to give her a choice; he wanted to pump every last drop of seed down her throat, but he wouldn't. Grinding his teeth, he managed to speak. Barely.

"I'm gonna come." He thrust in. "If you don't want..." He pulled out. "To swallow—"

Piper's fingers curled around the base of his shaft, her other hand cupped his sac and squeezed, and that hot, wet, glorious mouth pulled him deeper. She swirled her tongue, tugged on his balls, and sucked his orgasm from him. Scalding liquid lanced his cock, and fired through his length like a flaming arrow. Her throat closed around the sensitive gland as she gulped down the first spurt. Nate pulled back; he wanted the rest of his come to land on her tongue so she could taste him. Twice more he erupted into her before he pulled out completely.

He let go of her hair with one hand and fisted his pulsing erection. With a punishing grip, he milked the last of his release onto her lips. The creamy white fluid splashed her swollen red mouth and Nate would remember the way she looked, marked with his sperm, for the rest of his life. Her tongue lashed out, licked at the globs he'd sprayed on her face, and Nate's eyes nearly crossed. Sam groaned and leaning forward took her mouth with his. They kissed in a frenzy as Sam ate Nate's come from Piper's lips.

The blood leaving his cock stopped and surged back into the re-inflating organ. Seeing Sam and Piper kiss, swapping his come like it was the richest chocolate in the world, drove him back to aroused and ready to roll in seconds. He wanted her again. Both of them, wanted a piece of the action currently going on in front of him. Bending at the waist, he slid his mouth over Piper's cheek. He remembered her freaking out earlier when the three of them had shared a kiss, and he wanted to ease in, not spook her. But he needn't have worried; they turned toward him, both seeking his lips with theirs.

Slick and hot, tongues stroked and teased. They both pushed into his mouth and he sucked hard, pulling them closer to him. Piper moaned and Sam growled. An answering growl rumbled in Nate's chest and he thrust his tongue out to seek the recesses of Sam's mouth. She joined him, at first tentative, but soon she demanded with equal force. Together, they devoured Sam and all he had to offer. And then it was Piper's turn. Turning their attention to her, he and Sam licked and stroked, sucked and nipped until she thrashed about on the bed.

During the kiss, they'd moved. Piper still lay on her back, but he and Sam each draped along her sides, and both had a leg pushed between hers, their cocks humping into her hips. Their hands roamed, tangling together as all three of them sought to touch every inch of available skin. Nate squeezed a breast, tweaked a nipple. He trailed his fingers lower, over her ribs, down her stomach, and onto the hot slick cunt Sam had just fucked. His fingers were instantly coated with her cream and he delved deeper, slid a finger into her tight hole, and used his thumb to press on her clit.

Piper's nails clawed at his back, and he curled his hand and added another finger to the first. He pumped them in and out while keeping the pressure up on her clit. Sam's hand joined his, and they each hooked a foot around her calves and dragged her legs wider. She was so fucking wet Sam easily pushed his fingers in beside Nate's. They worked her mercilessly, and soon had her racing up another peak. In tandem they stroked and teased, driving her wild but not allowing her to reach the final summit. Torturing Piper only tortured Nate. His balls ached and his cock throbbed.

He wanted to be buried in her body again, wanted to slam his length inside the tight sheath he currently had his fingers in. He pumped his hips against her thigh; pre-come oozed and slicked both of them with his need. His mouth found its way to her breast and he latched onto her nipple, drew the hard point past his teeth, and trapped it there. She moaned and arched, her back lifting from the bed. More of her supple flesh filled him. With a groan he let the bud leave his lips with a pop.

He wanted to be inside her, wanted to fuck her cunt and

then take her ass, but she wasn't ready for that. Not the way he'd need to take her. He'd have to settle for her cunt, and let Sam take her virgin ass and get her ready for him. He couldn't let her leave without taking every part of her. Nate wasn't gentle when it came to sex, and he both admitted and accepted it. He also stayed honest enough with himself to know that if Sam wasn't here, he'd take her anyway.

His level of need scared him, but he needed to please Piper, to make everything good for her, and Nate wondered what he'd gotten himself into. She drew out dark desires, ones he'd felt before, but along with the need to take all before him was the need to give, to be the best he could be for her, and if he wasn't the best, then he'd get it for her.

They'd opened a Pandora's Box. Her innocence called to him, her willingness humbled him, and her demands inspired him to do more. *Be* more.

"I need to be inside you," he whispered in her ear.

"Yes." She spoke against his neck, her warm breath fanning out to shiver over his skin.

Sam handed him a condom already out of the packet and Nate leaned away from them, kicked away the briefs caught around one ankle, and put the protection on. He shuddered as he slid the latex down his erection. Before he could roll back on top of Piper, she came over him, straddled his hips, and with one hand, guided his straining cock to her opening. Inch by slow inch she descended. She rocked her pelvis, each slide back and forth taking him deeper. By the time she'd sunk to the hilt, sweat beaded on his brow, covered his chest, and breath wheezed from his lungs in ragged bursts.

Nate had never been as open, never felt so connected to another person before. This was different from what he and Sam had. Deep thoughts fled as Piper hastened the pace. She rode him now. Lifting up. Plunging down. In ever increasing speed, she slid along his length, her body sucking at his with every pass. He reached up and palmed her breasts, let them bounce in his hands as she drove them both toward orgasm. Sam's hand stole between them, his fingers searching for that tight bundle of nerves at the apex of her thighs. Piper moaned, lost her rhythm, and fell forward as his friend's fingers found their target.

He wrapped his arms around her, his hands traveling over her back and down to cup her ass. The change of angle and speed ramped up the race to the finish line. But Nate didn't want it to end yet; he needed Sam to be with them. Looking over her shoulder, he caught his friend's gaze. They didn't need words. Sam knew what he wanted, what he needed. With his hands splayed over Piper's ass, Nate held her still while he drove his cock up into her over and over. Sam moved out of sight and the scrape of a drawer opening echoed in the room.

His thrusts slowed, long and deep, as he altered the ride of her pussy along his shaft to maximize her pleasure without sending her over the edge. She lowered her head to his shoulder, her lips playing with the side of his neck. Sam moved back between Nate's outstretched legs, and Nate felt his fingers, cold with lube, brush against his balls as he began to work a finger over Piper's anus. Her body clutched at his, her inner muscles clamping down at Sam's invasion.

"Relax." He kissed her temple. "Let Sam in, Piper."

"Oh God." Her breathless cry followed Sam's push forward.

"Breathe deep, baby, let it out, and relax." He tried to soothe her as he held her still, his cock buried inside her. "It'll feel great after the initial sting, Piper, I promise."

He could feel Sam slowly pushing as she breathed out. Her body opened, and Nate felt his friend's finger press into his shaft through the thin membrane separating her two channels.

They began to move, short, gentle strokes in and out of her body. Sam's other hand slipped between them to play with her clit and Piper melted, her body giving way and allowing them to probe deeper, harder, faster. In no time, she began driving her hips back into them. Nate concentrated on keeping his control. Sweat dripped down the side of his face and his muscles strained for release.

Piper moaned and threw her head back as Sam pushed a second finger into her tight passage. The glide of Piper's soft flesh and Sam's hard fingers on his cock nearly set him off, but he clenched his jaw and tried to think of anything except the sensations flowing through him. She bit her lower lip, her white teeth sinking into the plump red curve. Nate surged up, locked his lips to hers, and took her mouth like he wanted to take her cunt. Hard and fast he probed inside with his tongue. He wasn't sure how he kept the rhythm of his thrusts even and slow but he did.

"Oh God, that feels..." she panted into his mouth.

"It's good, right?" He licked her lips, her teeth. "Imagine how good it'll feel when it's Sam's cock in your ass, Piper."

She shuddered and her pussy walls fluttered along his length.

"You want to feel Sam fuck your ass, don't you, Piper?"

"Ooh..." Her hips bucked, drove her pussy back hard on to both of them.

"I want more than anything to be your first, Piper." Nate pressed his mouth to hers. "But I can't give you what you need your first time. I can't go slow. Can't make it good for you. Sam's thicker than me, but he'll go easy, I won't. *Can't*. After he's fucked you and made you ready, it'll be my turn. I'll thrust into your gorgeous ass and fuck you hard. I want you too much to be gentle, Piper."

She moaned, nipped at his mouth, his chin, his jaw.

"Will you let Sam fuck you? Let him fill your tight hole while I'm buried in your cunt?"

"Ooh..."

Sam had three fingers in her ass now, Nate could feel them cupping his shaft inside her, the combination rapidly driving him insane. "Yes or no, Piper. We need to hear you say it." He wouldn't last much longer; they needed to know now.

Her hands curled around his biceps, her short nails digging into his skin. "Yes, God yes."

7

HOW COULD a man telling her he couldn't be the first to fuck her ass because he couldn't make it good for her be the sweetest thing any guy had ever said to her? She stared into Nate's eyes, saw the truth of his words in the dark depths, and knew this was more than just fucking her. The way he looked at her, looked right inside her. A shiver rippled in her belly.

This wasn't meant to be more. They were just supposed to give each other pleasure, a mutual enjoyment of a fantasy without any strings. Piper's chest tightened as the first knots pulled together. Closing her eyes, she tried to block out everything but the sensations bombarding her body.

She could feel Sam crowding behind her, the head of his cock pressing against her newly stretched opening. Nate's arms came around her, and he tucked her against his chest as Sam began to push in. Her muscles clenched, the burn already greater than when his fingers had been inside her. He pressed farther and she tensed more.

"Relax." Nate's fingers caressed her back. "Breath deep, let it out slow, bear down when you do."

Oh God! "It burns, I can't..."

"It's alright, Piper, just relax, breathe. I'm not moving any further. Not until you're ready," Sam whispered in her ear. He leaned over her, his arms straight, the muscles straining as they held up his weight, and held still while waiting for her to adjust to the new experience.

Cocooned by them, by their heat, by their concern, Piper felt more cherished than she ever had in her life. Her family's love had smothered her, but these two men, virtual strangers, made her feel secure, safe to be who she was, take what she wanted. She'd made a huge miscalculation when agreeing to have sex with them. They'd said no strings, but Piper suddenly found herself bound to them in a way she could never undo.

Her body was one big flame. The burn in her ass expanded to engulf her. It didn't hurt like she'd expected. Once the bulbous head of Sam's cock had slipped past the ring of muscle at her opening, she'd breathed easier and he'd slid right in up to his balls. She could feel his sac pressing into her, bumping against Nate's. Nerve endings never before stimulated burst to life, sending foreign sensations off in every direction.

No one moved for a heartbeat, the enormity of the moment not lost on any of them. Nate broke the stillness, pulling out until just the head of his cock remained inside her. Then he pushed back in and Sam retreated. Slowly. In and out. Out and in. A shudder racked her, a groan tearing from her throat.

It wasn't pleasure that sliced through her, not the kind she'd ever experienced, but it wasn't pain either. Each thrust ricocheted through her torso, and Sam's cock filling her back passage made her feel full to the point of exploding.

They drove into her, pulled out of her, dragging across sensitized tissues with devastating results. Her whole body buzzed like a live wire. The fine hairs on her arms stood on end and goose bumps covered her from head to toe. Each push in tangled with a pull out in a confusing collision of sensations Piper had no idea how to deal with. She couldn't move, couldn't join their rhythm because they were contradictory. All she could do was lay pinned between them and enjoy the ride.

The sharp sting of pain had long gone, but the burn of stretched muscles remained, adding a bite to the pleasure coursing through her blood, zapping over her nerves. Sam slid his hands between her and Nate to cup her breasts, pinch her nipples. Nate's fingers burrowed under her thigh and zeroed in on her clit. She rocked between them as they continued to pump into her. Heat blazed, starting in her clit and vibrating out until it hit her core and detonated in a fireball of piercing pleasure.

Piper's body bucked, every muscle clamping down, trapping both men inside her. For one second neither could move in or out, but then the wave rolled over and they surged in together. She screamed, the sound flung from her body on a breath of fire. Every inch of her was incinerated in a blinding orgasm. Sam squeezed her breasts hard and drove into her ass like never before. He froze, buried to his balls, and warmth pooled around his invading cock. Nate jerked under her, his length darting in and out as he too lost the fight and came with a grunt.

Heat bathed her lower belly as they emptied their bodies into hers. She wanted that warmth to spread, wanted it to seep inside her until it became part of her. The thought scared her. Piper was far from stupid and knew going without protection could mean all kinds of complications, but she wanted to do it anyway.

Sam inched his way out of her, the slide of his deflating cock sending aftershocks through her ass. As he finally pulled free and her muscles shrank back, a mild ache filled the void he'd left inside her. She groaned with the unfamiliar discomfort.

"Are you okay? I didn't hurt you?" Sam kissed her shoulder, her cheek. "Stay there and let me get a cloth to clean you up."

She tried to lift off Nate, but his arms tightened around her.

"Uh-uh. Stay right where you are until Sam gets back."

Piper relaxed against Nate's chest. His heart beat beneath her ear, and the rhythm and her body's exhaustion lulled her into a light sleep. The swipe of a warm cloth between her legs jerked her awake fully. She turned her head and looked over her shoulder to see Sam cleaning her with a washcloth. A towel sat on the bed beside him and he dried her carefully after wiping clean every square inch of her pussy, ass, and thighs. Nate's cock was no longer inside her and she had no idea when he'd slipped free.

Sam bent forward, bringing his face close to her groin. She tried to close her legs but he held her open and continued his perusal. Squirming, Piper buried her face in Nate's neck to hide her embarrassment.

"Is she okay?"

Nate's words had her head snapping up, her gaze darting back to look at Sam.

"A little red in places." He brushed a finger over her anus and she flinched.

"Sore, baby?" Nate asked.

She shook her head. "No. Not really." Sam grazed her puckered hole again and no matter how much she tried she couldn't stop herself from wincing. "A little sensitive, that's all."

"Maybe we should run the tub?"

"No, I'm fine." Piper covered her mouth as a yawn broke free. "Just need to rest for a bit and then I'll leave." Her final words slurred as sleep took hold.

"Leave? I don't think so. You're staying right here with us." Sam patted her ass.

"Nope, no leaving now." Nate's hand massaged the muscles in her neck.

Piper barely had enough energy to breathe, never mind comment, so she gave in to the drowsiness creeping in.

SAM HELD Piper in his arms while Nate went to clean up. She slept peacefully against him, her warm breath ruffling the hairs on his chest. The soft snores whistling over her slightly parted lips made him smile and hold her tighter. They were in deep.

No strings?

Bullshit.

There were plenty of them. Enough to cover a string quartet for life. Sighing, he closed his eyes and tried to think about what to do next.

He couldn't let her go, and he figured Nate would feel the same way. Sam had seen the look in his friend's eyes when they'd taken her together. No matter how much either of them protested otherwise, Piper had gotten way under their skin. The question was had they managed to burrow under hers?

And even if they had, would any sane woman agree to have a relationship with two men?

The bed dipped as Nate crawled up next to him. He brought the blanket with him and flipped it over Piper before moving in beside them. Sam opened his eyes and turned his head to find Nate staring at him.

"We're fucked, aren't we?"

Nate's question brought images of what they'd just done

with Piper to mind, but Sam knew that wasn't what his friend referred to.

Another sigh left his chest. "Yeah." He smoothed his hand down her spine but his touch didn't disturb her. "Especially if she wants those no strings we talked about."

"Jesus." Nate moved closer and curled his chest along Piper's back so they cradled her between them. "So what do we do?"

"Fucked if I know. This isn't anything like I expected."

"That makes two of us."

"Three."

They both stilled at the sound of Piper's sleepy voice.

"You're awake?" Sam asked.

"Just."

She didn't move, and her breathing remained long and even. If Sam hadn't been able to feel her heart beat increase against his chest, he would have thought she was talking in her sleep.

"Can we sleep on it? I don't want to miss this conversation and I'm so tired." Her lips brushed his chest as she yawned. "You guys sure know how to wear a girl out."

Sam laughed. "I'm not exactly full of energy right now." He patted her butt. "I think it's you that's worn me out."

"Good." She yawned again. "Go to sleep then."

"If we go to sleep, do you promise to be here in the morning?" Nate asked.

"As much as I'd like to run far away right now, I won't."

Nate kissed the top of her head. "I'm taking you at your word, but if you break it, I'll hunt you down and drag you back."

Sam felt Piper's lips curve against his chest. "Nathan the Neanderthal."

"Where you're concerned, yes."

"Sleep."

"Are you comfortable?" Sam asked.

"Mmm." She snuggled in closer.

Nate rolled over onto his belly and draped an arm over Piper's back, his fingers brushing Sam's nipple. He shuddered, the small nub still sensitive after their earlier activities. Glancing at Nate, he wondered just how they'd make this work. Not that he knew if Piper would give them a chance, but Sam couldn't help the hope building inside him. Hope that they'd found the missing piece that made everything else fit.

One thing Sam did know for sure was that she made everything else slot into place, and for the first time in over five years, he thought he understood what flowed between him and Nate. He loved him. As a friend, as a business partner, as a lover. And now, with Piper in the equation, he loved Nate as the man who would love her equally. Jesus. What the hell was he thinking? He couldn't be talking love and Piper. They hardly knew her; they knew nothing about her past. And if they were to have a future, they needed to know everything.

"Sam?" Her sleepy voice broke into his thoughts.

"Yeah," he murmured, mindful of Nate snoring next to them.

"Go to sleep. I can hear your mind ticking from here."

He smiled, kissed her forehead, and settled back on the pillow. "Night, Piper."

"Night, Sam."

NATE LAY ON HIS SIDE, his head propped on his hand, and watched the woman next to him sleeping.

The sun just peeked over the horizon, and the golden rays filled the room with a glow that sparkled along Piper's creamy skin. She wasn't pale, but she wasn't tanned like Sam or dark like him. He trailed his fingertips down her arm and admired the contrast of his darker skin against her paler tone.

"You'll stare holes in me if you're not careful."

He glanced up at her face and found her watching him. "Morning."

She smiled. "Morning."

"Sleep well?"

"Like a baby." She looked over her shoulder. "Where's Sam?"

"He ducked downstairs to put the coffee on. We'll get nothing sensible out of him until he's had at least three cups."

"Should we get up and join him?"

"No, he'll be back in a minute with his first cup." He pushed the sheet covering her a little lower until one smooth creamy swell of breast was revealed, and he itched to lean over and kiss it. "Unless you want a cup too."

"No, but I do want to use the bathroom." She smiled sheepishly and her cheeks turned pink.

"It's through that door there." He indicated the door behind him.

"Umm..." Her tongue poked out to lick her bottom lip and Nate groaned at the sight. "I don't have any clothes on."

"I know."

Silence followed his comment—a void in which Piper squirmed beneath the covers.

"Well I can't go wandering around naked!"

"Sure you can. No one can see you. We face the ocean."

"You can see me."

"Baby, I've seen every inch of you already. You don't have to hide from me."

"B-but—"

"Piper, even if you put clothes on, I'm going to tear them off the second you get back."

"Oh."

Before she could stop him, Nate grabbed the covers and threw them off the bed, leaving her laying there in all her naked glory. With a squeal, she rolled off the side of the mattress and darted across the room. He watched her perfect ass until she closed the door behind her, hiding all that luscious flesh from view. Damn. The minute she got back he was going to bend her over and fuck that ass of hers liked he'd promised last night.

"Where's Piper?" Sam walked in carrying a tray he placed on the dresser.

"What the hell have you got there?"

"Coffee."

"I don't want coffee."

"From the look of it you want Piper." Sam flashed his trademark grin, and Nate frowned.

"And you don't?"

"Never said that."

Water ran behind the bathroom door and Sam turned toward it.

"She's not showering, is she?"

"No, why? Want to wash her back for her?"

"Hell yeah. I woke up from a dream where we had her in the shower, all dripping wet and slippery." Sam swallowed and the front of his boxers tented over his erection.

Nate groaned. "Jeez, now there's an image."

The door opened and Piper stepped out with a towel wrapped around her, the end tucked in between her breasts. Nate growled and jumped off the bed. "What did I tell you about putting clothes on?"

"This is a towel, not clothes, and if Sam's allowed to cover up, then so am I." She raised her chin.

"Oh, I can fix that." Sam shucked his pants. "There. Drop the towel."

Piper's mouth opened and her jaw worked, but no words came out. With a huff, she walked toward them, threw the towel aside, and climbed back on the bed. Nate grinned and crawled across the mattress.

Sam came around the other side and together they stalked her.

"Now, about that ass fucking I owe you."

8

PIPER'S HIPS bucked with the orgasm rolling through her. Nate ate at her pussy like a starving man, lapping at her cream as it poured from her body. Sam stroked and suckled her breasts, pulled at her puckered nipples with his teeth. Hands and mouths worshiped her until she cried for more, begged them to take her—pleaded with them to stop the delicious torture.

Nate thrust his fingers in and out of her pussy and tongued her clit. The plug in her ass no longer burned. Instead it stretched and filled her, sent ribbons of heat through her core. She never would have guessed the pleasure one could get from anal sex. Her first time had been intense, a little pain with the ecstasy, but this time the sensations radiating out from her anus clawed at her insides until she craved something bigger. Piper lost her breath as the last wave of her release crashed over her.

Sam's mouth left her breast and she whimpered in protest. Limp from her orgasm, they easily turned her over and arranged her to their liking. Nate shoved two pillows under her belly and pulled her to her knees, her ass sticking up in the air, an open invitation. Her eyelids fluttered, their weight almost too heavy to lift. Sam sat in front of her, his legs spread on either side of her body and his cock inches from her mouth. Piper's mouth watered, and her tongue darted out to lick her lips. She wanted to taste him.

"Suck his cock," Nate muttered in her ear. "I want to see that sexy mouth stretched wide and Sam's cock driving deep."

Her belly clutched. The heat so recently doused instantly flamed to life. Piper pressed back into Nate's body, her ass cradled by his hips, his length sliding between her cheeks, pressing on the plug.

"That's right, I'm gonna fuck your ass while I watch you suck Sam off." He licked up her neck and nipped her earlobe, sending an electric dart down her spine to land in her pussy.

She moaned, rocked back against him and opened her mouth for Sam who wiggled forward until his length stood tall directly under her lips. Piper swirled her tongue over the head and collected the bead of pre-come from the slit before sucking him in. Drawing hard, she pulled him inside her. He was wider than Nate, but she soon worked out a rhythm to suit them both. Taking him to the back of her throat, she swallowed around him, his hips bucked, and a groan echoed above her. As she drew back, she scraped her teeth lightly until she reached the sensitive spot just under the crown, teasing with her tongue, then she sucked on the end like a lollipop.

Sam growled, tangled his hands in her hair, and shoved forward. Relaxing, Piper let him drive to the back of her throat again. In and out, suck and lick. Saliva ran down her chin but she didn't care. All she cared about was Sam's cock and the way it made her feel to have him fucking her mouth. She rested on her elbows, one hand wrapped around the base of his shaft; the other cupped his sac and played with his balls. He sped up, plunging with long strokes, all the way in, all the way out.

Consumed with the head job she was giving Sam, Pip almost forgot about Nate. She soon remembered when Nate began removing the butt plug from her ass. Her body flamed, clenched around the rubber probe trying to stop it from escaping.

"Relax, let it out. I promise to replace it with something better." He soothed her, brushed his palm over the curve of her hip, and pulled the plug from her tight opening.

Spasms racked her, her inner muscles convulsing in reaction to the stimulation. Piper moaned around Sam's flesh when Nate spread cool lube over the knot of puckered skin. Sam stilled, his thumbs caressing her cheeks as Nate moved in to press against her. She whimpered. She knew he would be rough, and a part of her longed to take him that way, but a slither of fear snaked through her belly.

Anxiety tightened her muscles, and both men tried to reassure her in their own way. Nate cupped her ass cheeks, circling his fingers across each curve. Again a moan slipped from her mouth as the head of his cock breached her clenching hole.

Piper dropped her hands from Sam's body and gripped the sheet in her fists. With Sam's cock in her mouth, she breathed through her nose and willed her body to relax. Sam started to move, short, sharp jerks of his hips to push and pull his cock between her lips. Nate leaned over her, his chest making contact with her spine. From shoulders to thighs, he covered her. He reached around her stomach, his fingers strumming their way over her hypersensitive skin, and worked his way to her pussy. Cupping her mound, he curled his hand and pressed on her engorged flesh.

Gasping for breath, Pip was overwhelmed by splintering nerve endings as her body gave way and Nate surged forward, taking her in one hard thrust. He retreated, drove into her, retreated, and drove in again. Each slam of his cock into her willing depths shoved her onto Sam's length. Over and over, Nate pounded into her. She couldn't think, could only feel, and she felt possessed. Sam moved in time with Nate.

With every lunge into her, they grunted, their hands and fingers digging in to her hips and head.

They held her, took what they wanted from her in the race to find release. She should feel used, their actions a turn off; instead her arousal skyrocketed, and she wanted to scream for them to fuck her harder. Faster. Take all of her. Whatever they wanted. Nate's demands on her body were answered eagerly; with a desperation she'd never experienced, Piper sought more. Hollowing her cheeks, she sucked Sam's cock, letting him dictate the speed and depth. For this moment in time she would be theirs to use, to seek their ultimate pleasure from.

And with their pleasure she would receive hers.

HE HAD to hold on a little longer, just a little more. Nate clenched his jaw, fought the orgasm rushing at him. Piper was close too; he could feel her channel quivering around him, knew with just a little more...

She exploded under him. Her ass clamped around his cock in a punishing grip that held him still until her muscles unlocked and the convulsions started.

Squeeze, release. Squeeze, release. And then he was done.

Lightning shot up his spine, and fire streaked through his balls and shaft. Jet after jet of come blasted from his body to fill the latex shield he wore. They bucked and thrashed together, their movements erratic—uncontrolled. Nate threw his head back, eyes closed, and roared. Blind with pleasure, his instincts took over, and he rammed in and out of her with wild abandon.

Sam's shout mixed with the drumbeat pounding in Nate's

ears, and he opened his eyes to see his friend spilling into Piper's mouth. Come leaked from around Sam's cock to slide down her chin. Nate collapsed, his sweaty chest plastered to her back, and his straining arms shook as they struggled to hold up his weight. He didn't have the energy to pull out of her yet. His breath came in ragged pants, and he rested his face in the curve of her neck, watching as she licked Sam's softening shaft clean.

Nate knew he had to move; he didn't want to crush her beneath him, and it was a definite possibility that he would when his arms finally gave out. He kissed her neck, nibbled her jaw, following the line until he reached her mouth. She tilted her head toward him and tangled her tongue with his. Sam's scent and taste was all over her; their combined smell and flavor drove him crazy, and his cock pulsed within the tight walls of her ass.

Her eyes widened. "Again?" she whispered against his lips.

He shook his head. It wasn't that he couldn't or didn't want to take her again, but that he shouldn't.

She had to be sore. Nate felt guilty about fucking her the way he had. He'd been rough, and even though he'd seen to her pleasure, he still wasn't quite comfortable with what he'd done.

"You didn't hurt me, Nate." She rested her forehead on his. "It's been the most amazing experience of my life. Yesterday. Last night. This morning. I've loved every second of it, and as soon as I get my breath back I'd like to do it all over again."

"God. You're gorgeous, you know that?" Sam cupped her cheek, turned her head until she looked at him. "Nate has issues with the way he demands. No matter how willing the *demandee*, guilt always rides his back when he's done."

Nate shuddered and slowly withdrew from Piper's ass. Her walls sucked at him, grabbed at his retreating flesh, sending fire licking over his skin. She dropped to the mattress as he finally pulled free, a gust of air spilling from her chest.

"Oh Lord. I don't think I'll even move again." The bedding scrunched up under her face muffled Piper's words.

Sam laughed. "That's okay, I'll be stuck right here beside you." He inched down the bed next to her.

Nate removed the condom from his spent cock and crawled off the bed. On wobbly legs he made his way to the bathroom to take care of the clean up. In minutes he returned to the bed, washcloth in hand, and attended to Piper. He tossed a second cloth at Sam. She didn't move, and the little moans coming from her throat told him some places were more tender than others. Guilt tugged at his gut.

"I'm sorry I hurt you." He planted a kiss on her right butt cheek.

"Nate, you didn't hurt me." She rolled over, causing him to move out of the way. Sitting up, Piper placed both hands on his face and stared into his eyes. "I'm a little tender, but in the last few hours I've used muscles never used before. There's bound to be some aches and a bit of stiffness."

He wanted to believe her. And he did in a way, but it warred with the need to protect her, comfort her, and please her. The desire to be a better person for her. To show her how much he loved...

Wow! Where did that come from? He couldn't love her. Sure he lusted after her, even now when they'd fucked more times than he had in the last six months in the space of a few hours he still wanted her with a need that was raw in its intensity.

Could he love her? The idea flowed through his mind, sat comfortably, and filled him with the knowledge that yes, he *could* love her, had probably already started falling for her. This complicated things. He thought of the "no strings" agreement and knew he'd use everything in his power to make sure she wanted to be tied to them.

"There are strings." Nate couldn't hold back. He needed to know when to fight, how to fight, and he wouldn't know that until he worked out how she felt, what she wanted.

Piper kissed his lips, then turned to look at Sam, who leaned against the headboard. Nate's gaze met his friend's and he saw fear to match his own. But also determination. Sam would fight beside him for a chance at whatever this thing with Piper was.

With two fingers on her chin, he bought her head around so she faced him again.

"I have no idea what this is, why this is, but what I do know is it doesn't end here." He glanced at Sam. "If you're willing to give us a chance, we want to see where we can go. Whether there's something special between us."

"Okay."

"Okay? Just like that?"

She smiled at him. "Do you honestly think I don't feel it? I don't understand it, but I know I can't walk away yet."

"So you're in this with us?" Sam asked.

Nate knew what Sam was doing. In one sentence, he made sure Piper understood they were all involved.

"Yes." She reached over and grabbed Sam's hand, giving it a gentle squeeze. "All of us."

He blew out the breath he'd been holding. Leaning over, Nate added his hand on top of theirs. "All of us."

"I NEED SOMETHING FROM YOU BOTH."

Sam peered across the table at Piper and wondered what

else she could need. They'd satisfied her hunger, for food and for sex. What else could there be?

Nate chewed and swallowed the mouthful of lunch he just taken. "Anything. It's yours."

"You don't know what I want yet." She raised one eyebrow. "Maybe I want a kidney."

"It's yours."

There was no hesitation in Nate's words, and even though Sam hadn't spoken a word he had to agree with Nate. Anything she wanted.

Piper watched Nate carefully before turning her gaze on him. "What about you, Sam?"

"Name it."

She drew in a deep breath and let it out slowly. Her uncertainty rocked him and a hard ball formed in the pit of his stomach.

"I want to see you together."

He stared at her, confused. "We are together."

"No, *together* together."

Nate sat up straight. "You want us to...while you watch?"

"No." She licked her lips and Sam's groin tightened. "I want one of you to fuck me while being fucked by the other. I don't care who does who, but I want to *see* you together, all of us together."

Her words rushed out, not a breath of air between them, and Sam smiled. She was nervous, but she did what they'd asked her to do. They wanted her to make demands of them like they did of her. It looked like she'd finally built up the courage.

He pushed his chair back and stood up. "Now?"

"What? No, no...um...whenever."

Sam laughed. "You finally got the courage to ask for something, Piper, don't back down now."

Walking around the table, he pulled her chair back and reached for her hand. With a tug, he yanked her to her feet. "Now."

"Okay." She shivered in his grasp.

Chair legs scraped across the tile floor as Nate surged from his seat. "We'll leave the dishes for later." He strode from the room, leaving them to follow.

Sam held Piper's hand and walked toward the stairs. "You know we would have done this eventually. We're just too caught up in the enjoyment of you at the moment, but we never would have hidden this part of us from you."

She leaned her head on his shoulder. "I know, but I need to see this now. I'm worried about the way I'll feel when I'm not the center of attention, when one of you is."

The idea he and Nate together physically would concern her sent a ripple of worry through his heart. "Can't blame you for worrying, and I'm glad you trust us enough to voice those concerns. I need to know you'll do that all the time, Piper. If we do anything, say anything, that you don't like, I want you to tell us."

"Okay." She pulled free of his hand and raced up the stairs. "You're taking too long," she yelled over her shoulder as she darted for their room.

Sam took off after her. When he entered the bedroom, she and Nate were already naked and rolling on the bed. Jesus, they couldn't even wait two seconds? He tore off his shirt, pushed down his shorts, and joined them.

No one made the decision. In the end it just came down to letting it flow. Sam watched Nate surge into Piper's pussy. He let them go for a few strokes before moving in behind them. With the ease of long practice, and an extra-lubricated condom, Sam slid into Nate's ass, the tight clamp of his friend's body a welcome grip. They moved in counterpoint. Nate thrust into

Piper as Sam pulled out of him. Sam drove into Nate as he retreated from Piper. The slow rock of hips was nothing like the frenzy of their previous lovemaking.

He wouldn't deny it any more. The emotion filling his chest was love. Neither of them were ready to hear it, and Sam certainly wasn't ready to say it, but he could show it. Wrapping his arms around Nate, he sought Piper's hands. Entwining their fingers, he held onto her as he made love to Nate, as Nate made love to her. Their pace picked up, their moans growing as they pushed each other on. Sam flexed his hips harder, and Nate answered by clenching his muscles tighter. His balls ached, throbbing with the need to come.

"I won't last long," he said with a growl.

"Almost...there." Piper panted.

Nate bucked between them. "Harder."

Sam did as asked and drove his body into Nate's as hard as he could. Piper cried out and thrashed under them. Sam felt the ripples of her orgasm through Nate as his friend lost the battle and came. The hot sheath surrounding his cock gripped him like molten steel. His sac pulled up, shoved his balls up beneath his shaft, and pushed the boiling come through his length.

He arched back, plunged deep inside Nate, and held still as he emptied out. Spasms shook him. From his head to his toes, Sam pulsed with his release. Sweat dripped from his body onto Nate, and his muscles turned to liquid. Collapsing forward, he lay sprawled over both of them.

"Jesus. Get...off...me..." Piper panted. "Too...heavy."

With what little strength he had left, Sam slipped from Nate's body and fell to the bed beside them. Nate soon followed, falling on the other side of Piper.

"Good God," Nate murmured.

Sam smiled. "I know. I think I'm dead. I can't feel my toes."

Piper laughed. "Seeing how you're numb, you can be on the bottom next time then."

"As long as there is a next time, I don't care where I am," Sam said.

"I'll second that." Nate raised his hand.

"All in favor, say aye," Piper added.

Three ayes echoed around the room right before they burst out laughing. And Sam knew that even with the future being unsure, they stood a damn good chance of making this work.

EPILOGUE

PIPER PUSHED through the glass door into the scorching summer heat. Her second summer in Sydney proved just as hot as the first. Picking the table closest to the beach, she pulled out a chair and sat. It was time for her daily dose of her *Bondi Beach Boys*.

Of course she'd already had one dose first thing that morning. She grinned. Oh yes, she was a good girl and took her medicine regularly.

In twelve months, lots of things had changed. Her business had grown, and she was thinking of bringing on an employee. And on a personal front, things had never looked better. Sam and Nate filled her days with love, and even with the extra effort needed for a relationship of three, Piper couldn't be happier. Well, maybe she could be.

She watched them walk up the beach, water running down their dark skin, dripping off their shorts. They didn't stop at the car, but kept walking until they stood right in front of her.

"What are you grinning at?" Nate asked.

"Oh nothing, just happy."

"I can think of a way I can make you happier." Nate waggled his eyebrows in an exaggerated suggestive leer.

Piper giggled. "Can you now?"

"Oh, most definitely yes." He leaned down and took her mouth with his. Thrusting his tongue deep, he devoured her.

Sam moaned, wrapped his hand around her arm, and pulled her from her seat. But Nate wouldn't let her mouth go and she quickly found herself pressed between two hot wet bodies.

Nate tore his mouth from hers, and his eyes swirled with lust, his nostrils flared.

"Fuck." Sam rubbed his cock against her ass. "Time to go home."

"I want you the second we get inside the house, Piper." Nate leaned his forehead on hers. "I want to feel your hot cunt around me while Sam fucks your ass. And I want to do it on the hood of the car."

Piper sucked in a breath. Oh yes, time to go home and have another dose of *Bondi Beach Boys*.

SAND, SURF AND SUNNIE

*For me because I had so much fun last time I wanted to bask
under the hot rays of a summer sun once more.
And as always, to the man who is my own personal sunshine.
Love ya, Babe!
Together forever.*

1

"FUCKING BASTARD."

Sunnie swung her arm in a wide arc and slammed the front door. The force rattled the walls and sent a gust of hot air sweeping through the hallway, lifting the hem of her dress.

"Stupid fucking rat!" Sunnie pushed her skirt down with one hand and threw her purse and keys in the general direction of the hall table with the other.

"Hey, Sunshine, date not go so well?"

Fuck! What the hell was Rand doing home? He and Z were supposed to be out tonight. Dammit, she wanted to lick her wounds in peace and quiet. Alone. Maybe she could ignore him and slink off to her—

"No point avoiding me. I'll just come out there and fetch you." Rand's voice echoed off the walls.

With a sigh, Sunnie kicked off her high heels and cursed herself a fool for going to so much trouble with her outfit. "Fucking rat bastard!"

"What was that?" Rand yelled but—much to Sunnie's relief —he didn't come out of the living room. *Yet.*

Shit! She wasn't going to be able to hide. Any minute Rand would follow through on his threat if she didn't show her face, and making a run for her bedroom wouldn't help. He'd only bash on her door then pick the flimsy lock to get in. It wouldn't be the first time he or Z had picked a locked door. That was the problem with sharing a house with your two best friends. There was no privacy.

"Sunshine?"

"Stop calling me that!" Sunnie stomped down the hall. Her bare feet made little impact against the hard tile surface but it was worth the effort just for the release of frustrated energy boiling inside her.

"Uh-oh. The date was *that* bad?"

Sunnie entered the living room to find Rand sprawled across the couch. His long, muscular body draped the leather cushions like a centerfold model, only with clothes on. Her insides stirred at the sight of all that male perfection. He held the TV remote in one hand and a beer in the other. She stalked over, plucked the bottle from his grasp and chugged down what was left. It was barely half full, but it was cold and wouldn't take much more for her to get a buzz going. She had nothing in her stomach, after all. Her dinner date had been a bust on more than one front.

"Whoa. Slow down there, Sunshine. You know you're a cheap drunk."

Drunk! That's exactly what she needed to be to forget her depressing, disastrous, nonexistent love life. "Got another one in the fridge? Never mind, stupid question. Of course you do." Sunnie headed for the kitchen.

Leather squeaked as Rand scrambled to get off the couch and follow her. "Sunnie, sweetie, it can't be that bad. You remember how horrible it was last time you got a little tipsy."

Sunnie threw a glare over her shoulder. "Believe me, that hangover has nothing on the shitty way I feel right now."

He grabbed her hand and pulled her to a stop. "Don't. You'll regret it tomorrow, Sunshine. Besides, he's not worth it."

"This isn't about him. It's about *me*! And stop calling me that!" Sunnie yanked her hand free and continued in the direction of beer-induced oblivion.

"You? What the hell?" Rand followed and scooted past to block her way. "What do you mean it's about you?"

Rand stood with his arms crossed over his broad chest, his imposing six foot two frame ramrod straight. He should have been menacing and she supposed he would be to someone who didn't know him as well as she did. Sunnie mimicked his stance. His gaze lowered, snagging on her breasts which, she noticed, were pushed up by her arms and threatening to spill over the top of her dress. *Great. Just great.* "Ahem."

A smile teased his lips as his gaze met hers once more. "Sorry, Sunshine, but those beauties are a definite distraction to anyone with a cock. Probably for some without, too."

"Rand!" Dammit, the last thing she needed was for him to start drooling over her girl bits. God! Her long-neglected libido would take Rand's attention and run with it. With a sigh she dropped her arms. "Can I please get a beer?"

One brown eyebrow arched as he studied her. "Fine. But no getting drunk."

"Spoilsport." Sunnie poked out her tongue as he stepped aside.

She thought he groaned, but a glance over her shoulder revealed him heading back to the living room, his gorgeous ass on perfect display in his well-worn denim shorts. Warmth curled in her lower belly, but Sunnie did what she always had when it came to any possible signs of arousal for either of her housemates. Ignored it.

Opening the refrigerator, she scanned the contents for something to eat. If she had any hope of keeping to Rand's *no getting drunk* decree she'd need something in her stomach to soak up some of the alcohol before it hit her bloodstream. She'd barely swallowed a bite of bread stick before her date had been ruined. Besides, a rummage in the fridge meant she could stall a little longer. She knew once she went back to the other room Rand would want full disclosure of her sucky evening.

There was nothing on the shelves except beer, half a carton of questionable milk, a block of fuzzy green cheese, and a plastic container with something that could have been edible at one time. Sunnie pulled out the vegetable drawer and instantly wished she hadn't. The smell was nauseating. Pinching her nose and breathing through her mouth, she shoved the drawer closed. Where was all the food she'd bought the other week? Rand and Z had obviously eaten them out of house and home—again—and as usual, not bothered to replace anything.

"Fucking men!"

"Did you say something?" Rand yelled.

"Do you want another beer?" Sunnie called in her sweetest voice.

"No. I'll share yours."

Damn him. He really was serious about the *no getting drunk* thing. Sunnie sighed and grabbed a beer. She spun on her heel and bumped the fridge shut with her hip before heading back to the inevitable third degree Rand would subject her to.

She found him in the same position as before, but as she approached he scooted up to rest against the sofa arm. One of his legs dropped to the floor while the other remained stretched out along the cushions. He patted the seat between his spread thighs.

"Come on, Sunshine, tell me all about the latest unworthy male in a long line of unworthy SOBs."

Sunnie's step faltered, her stomach clenched, and her bottom lip trembled. Her eyes stung, moisture rapidly pooling to blur her vision. "What's wrong with me?" The question slipped off her tongue before she could think better of it.

Rand dived off the couch. "Oh, no you don't. Golden rule number one—no crying over the SOBs." He wrapped his arms around her, tucking her against his chest.

Warmth surrounded her and—not for the first time—she cursed the fact she couldn't fall in love with him or Z. Why weren't there more men like them out there? But Rand was right; years ago after a particularly nasty bust up they'd made her promise to never cry over a guy again. Sniffing back her tears she tried to pull from Rand's embrace.

"Don't." He tightened his grip. "Just let me hold you a second longer."

Sighing, she leaned into him and soaked up the comfort he offered. For just a moment Sunnie allowed herself to absorb the carnal delight of being pressed to Rand's hard body. Her double D's were squashed into his chest and her nipples puckered at the contact. She gloried in the thrill his innocent hug delivered. At least, she did until she moved her hips and brushed against something hard. Something that wasn't his hip and certainly *wasn't* innocent.

Rand abruptly let her go and turned away. "Sit down, Sunshine. I'll be back in a sec. Gonna grab a beer after all."

Sunnie watched as he all but ran from the room. Okay, she may be emotionally strung out after her disastrous evening and pity-party frame of mind, but there was no way she'd misinterpreted the bulge in Rand's pants. What the hell was going on? First he's checking out her rack and now he's getting a boner from holding her? Dumbfounded, she lowered herself to the couch, her gaze glued to the doorway he'd disappeared through, and waited for him to return.

Even though Sunnie was dying to confirm Rand did have a hard-on she couldn't bring herself to check. The second he entered her line of sight she whipped her head around and stared at the muted television. None of the pictures flashing across the screen formed recognizable images to her unfocused eyes. Instead, like a preschooler's finger painting, each color smudged into the next until it resembled a kaleidoscope of shades in perpetual motion.

The couch dipped as Rand sat beside her and from the corner of her eye she saw him lift the leg closest to her and cross it over the other, hiding his groin area from view. Her eyeballs stung as she strained to turn them as far to the right as she could. It did no good. He'd blocked her visual access completely. Sunnie brought the beer in her hand to her lips. Cold metal clinked against her teeth and with a snarl she yanked it away and thrust it in Rand's direction.

"Open it." She frowned at the rude tone of her voice. "Please." The tacked-on courtesy did nothing to soften the demand.

Rand chuckled as he twisted off the bottle cap and handed the beer back. "You really are in a foul mood."

Sunnie didn't answer; there didn't seem to be anything to say. She *was* in a foul mood and, although she wanted to, she couldn't lay complete blame at the feet of her rat bastard date. No. This evening's debacle was just the last in a lifetime of disastrous attempts to find the man of her dreams. Her chest rose and fell on a heavy sigh as she slumped back against the couch.

"It couldn't have been that bad." Rand bumped his shoulder into hers. "Wanna tell me what happened? It might help."

She closed her eyes. "I'm not sure I want anyone to know the circumstances of this one."

"Oh, let me guess. The guy arrived naked with a one-inch dick hanging between his legs."

Beer fizzed up Sunnie's nose as she snorted with laughter. Covering her mouth so the rest of her mouthful didn't come spilling out, she tried to swallow. Humor quickly turned to distress when she choked on her drink. Rand plucked the bottle from her hand and placed it on the table while thumping her on the back in an attempt to help clear her airways. Managing to gulp down the beer, she gasped for breath.

"Jesus." Her chest heaved as she coughed out her words. "Way to kill me, Rand." With her breathing under control she spoke easier. "Not an image I wanted in my head, Brandon Davis."

"At least it made you laugh. Before you choked." He continued to pat her on the back. "You really should stop drinking, Sunshine. You can't handle booze at all."

"Hey!" Sunnie punched him in the arm. "I can handle a drink just fine. It's the nosy, annoying so-called friends that upset me."

"Ha!" He chucked her under the chin with his fist. "You love me and you know it."

"Of course I do." Sunnie reached over and grabbed her beer. She carefully took a sip and allowed the cool liquid to soothe her raw throat. "Doesn't mean I won't kill you in your sleep."

"Why are we killing Rand in his sleep?" Z asked from the doorway.

"Because he tried to kill me first. *Twice.*"

"Twice? Determined."

"First he tried to fry my brain with my own imagination and when that didn't work he relied on the tried-and-true method of choking." Next to her, Rand shook with the laughter he was unsuccessfully concealing behind his hand.

"I see he failed in both attempts. Do you want me to ring the cops and have him carted off?"

Sunnie eyed a now openly laughing Rand. "Mmm...no, I think a suitable punishment would be for him to order and pay for pizza."

"Hey! It's not my turn."

Sunnie poked Rand in the ribs with her index finger. "Shoulda thought of that before you tried to do me in."

"Paying for pizza seems a fair price for such a terrible crime." Z walked over to the couch and offered her his hand. "And it just so happens I picked up some of your favorite ice cream while shopping. Come and help me put the groceries away while Rand organizes dinner."

"You bought food?" Sunnie didn't resist as Z pulled her to her feet.

"Sure did." He curled his fingers through hers and towed her with him. "I've been making a list of what we've used in the last two weeks so that I could replace it. I know how it pisses you off to find the cupboards empty."

"Aw, my hero."

"That's fine, Z. You steal my girl with your promise of sweet dessert, but she'll be mine again the minute the pepperoni pizza gets here."

"Now, now. No need to fight over me. I'll let you share." Sunnie slammed into Z's back when he stopped dead in his tracks.

Z looked over his shoulder at Rand, eyebrows raised.

"She's tipsy. She doesn't mean what it sounds like."

"What? What don't I mean? What did I say?" Sunnie swiveled her gaze back and forth between her two friends.

"Christ." Z's grip tightened on her hand. "Come on, let's get this food put away before it goes off."

Before she could protest further, Z headed for the kitchen, tugging her with him. She glanced back at Rand and tried to interpret the twisted look on his face. Sunnie was immediately jolted from her thoughts when they entered the kitchen. The counters were covered in bags of shopping, and more lay scattered on the floor.

"Wow, Z. Did you buy the whole supermarket?"

"What? Oh." He shrugged. "I got two of everything so we wouldn't have to shop again so soon."

Sunnie stared at the person who looked like her best friend and wondered when the aliens had taken over. Neither of the guys ever purchased food without her dragging them to the shops. And with her kindergarten class being dismissed at three o'clock it was simpler for her to grocery shop on her own after work.

"Don't look at me like that."

"But you never do the shopping."

"Doesn't mean I'm not capable of doing it." Z moved over to pick up a bag. "It's just...you always beat us to it."

"Pizza's on the way." Rand stopped in the doorway. "Shit, Z. Did you leave anything on the shelves?"

"Ha-ha. Make yourself useful and put the cold stuff away."

"Um, I think we better clean out the fridge before we fill it. Other than the beer, there isn't one thing that doesn't need burning."

"Is that what the smell is?"

"Smell?" Sunnie looked at Rand.

"When I got my beer earlier there was a strange smell in there."

"God, Rand, you could smell that without opening the vegetable drawer and you didn't clean it?"

Rand ducked his head and walked over to the sink. "Maybe." He grabbed a roll of paper towels and the bottle of cleaner from the cupboard. "I'll do the fridge. You help Z with the rest."

Sunnie smiled at the grim look on Rand's face. Anybody would think he was off to the gallows. "I'll do it. You never get all the corners properly."

"Nope. I'm doing it. You can supervise if you want, but it's come to our attention that you've been doing the majority share of the cleaning over the years so I'm fixing that now."

"Okay, who are you two and what have you done with the real Brandon and Zeke?"

"Oh, we're all comedians this evening." Z handed her a bag. "Here, go put the bathroom stuff away."

She glanced in the bag and burst out laughing. "You bought tampons?"

Z blushed. "You're down to your last box."

"You checked?" Sunnie was astounded at Z's thoroughness.

"I checked every cupboard and drawer in the house." Z turned his back and busied himself with the contents of another bag, effectively ending the conversation.

Sunnie headed to the bathroom with the bag of supplies. Z hadn't missed anything. The bag contained everything from tampons to razor blades. He'd even bought the face moisturizer she preferred. She placed the last bottle of shampoo in the cupboard as Z came in.

"Here. Toilet paper." He dropped a packet of twenty rolls at her feet. "Might need to store half of them in the linen cupboard."

"Ya think?" Sunnie straightened up and turned towards him. "Why the sudden domestic proficiency?"

Z shrugged. "You've always done more than your share. It's time we chipped in."

"I've never complained about it."

"I know, but it's going to stop anyway."

"Why?"

"Because it was pointed out, not too kindly, that we take advantage of you. I didn't like the way that made me feel." He reached over and ran his fingertip down her cheek. "No one should ever take advantage of you, Sunshine."

Sunnie wasn't sure what to say to that. She wanted to know who was talking about them and exactly what had been said, but Rand interrupted by yelling down the hall.

"Pizza's here."

The beauty of living three doors down from a pizza shop was super-fast delivery service. They headed back to the kitchen where the pizzas were waiting. The smell of fresh-baked dough, rich tomato, and spicy meat filled the air, making her mouth water.

"I'm starving." She lifted the lid on the first box and pulled out a slice. Cheese stretched in an ever thinning line from the remaining pie as she raised the piece to her mouth. Flavor exploded on her tongue as she sank her teeth in. "Mmm...Yummy."

"One thing I've always loved about you, Sunnie—you're not afraid to eat and enjoy it." Z grabbed a slice and devoured half of it in one bite.

"Are we going to eat in here or do we want to take it in the living room and see what's on the TV?" Rand didn't bother waiting for an answer. He picked up the two boxes and headed out of the room.

"Guess I missed making that decision." Sunnie smiled. "I'll grab paper towels."

"I'll get the beers." Z shoveled the rest of his slice into his mouth and pulled open the fridge.

"Only two beers," Rand called out. "Sunnie's had enough already."

"Hey! I'm not drunk."

"No. And you're not going to be either," Rand yelled from the other room.

Sighing, Sunnie grabbed the roll of towel and trudged in Rand's wake, devouring her pizza as she went.

"Cheer up." Z caught up and bumped her elbow with his. "I'll let you have most of mine if you promise not to tell the fun police."

"I heard that and you just volunteered to hold her hair out of the toilet bowl."

Z laughed. "It won't come to that."

"You said that last time she drank."

Sunnie dropped the paper roll on the table beside the pizza and broke off another slice. "I'm perfectly capable of knowing my limits and stopping when I reach them."

"And *you* said that last time Z talked you into a drink." Rand reached out and curled his fingers around her wrist. "Sit and eat. We'll worry about your beer intake later."

She let him pull her down beside him. "So what's on the television?"

"Don't know." Z picked up the remote and began flicking channels as he sat on the floor. "Yell if you see anything good."

Several minutes later and a second run through of the evening's viewing proved there were slim pickings for a Friday night.

"Do we have any decent movies that we haven't watched a billion times?" Rand asked.

"Actually I picked up some new ones at the supermarket." Z pushed up from the floor. "I'll get one."

"Which one?" Sunnie asked. "Hey, and bring me back a beer."

Z returned and passed her a beer along with a movie case before walking over and slipping a disc into the player.

"*Footloose?*" She showed the cover picture to Rand. "The original with Kevin Bacon."

"What? No *Dirty Dancing?*" Rand smirked.

Z turned to look at them. "You wanna watch that instead? I got it too."

Sunnie and Rand sat in stunned silence for a second before they simultaneously burst into laughter. She laughed so much her sides hurt, and when she glanced up at Z the look on his face only made her laugh harder.

"I'm glad you both find my movie choices amusing. At least we know you'll have a good time." He turned back and fiddled with the machine. "Okay, we're set."

"We're really going to watch *Footloose?*" Rand asked.

"Hell yeah, it's a great movie." Z came over and sat next to Sunnie.

"Jesus, were we even born when it came out?" Rand asked.

"I remember watching it at a slumber party in my early teens and it was old then." Sunnie smiled at the memory. That night had been a revelation. The girl whose house they were sleeping at had three older siblings and they'd discovered some interesting magazines, clothes, and sex toys during the hours after dark.

"What has that silly grin on your face?" Z asked.

"I'm just reminiscing about the first time I watched this."

"Nuh-uh, that smile is more than a fond movie memory."

"Maybe. But I'm not telling you." She reached for the remote and pushed Play, switching the volume up at the same time.

"Fine. I don't want to know anyway." Z crossed his arms and exaggerated a pout.

Sunnie laughed. "You're a clown sometimes, you know that?"

"Knock it off you two. I'm trying to watch the movie," Rand said.

"Jeez, man, it's just the trailers. Gimme that." Z snatched the controller from Sunnie's hand. "Fast-forward this shit."

"Hey, I like watching those." Sunnie tried to grab the remote, but Z raised his arm up and back, out of reach.

Sunnie twisted toward him and with one hand on his thigh, braced her weight to lean across him, but no matter how far she stretched she couldn't get to the controller. For a few moments they jostled against each other and by the time she gave up the effort they were both breathing hard. She sagged against him and something dug into her stomach. A hard bulge pressed into her belly and she was certain Z wasn't wearing a belt buckle. Board shorts didn't need belts.

Drawing in a breath, she brought her gaze over to meet Z's. Rand had gone perfectly still beside them and at some point Z must have paused the movie, leaving the only sound in the room their labored breathing. Sunnie met Z's emotion-filled stare with confusion. She couldn't be sure what she read wasn't her own feelings reflected back, or wishful thinking. Her gaze dropped to his lips and the urge to kiss him streaked through her.

Shocked by her own desire, she carefully lifted herself off his lap and sat back, her gaze rising to meet Z's again. For what seemed like hours but could only be seconds, they stared at each other. It seemed as though time froze and, if the strident ring of a phone hadn't broken the awkward silence, they may have remained that way forever.

"Gotta get that." Z stood as though his pants suddenly caught fire. "It'll be work."

He strode from the room in much the same way Rand had

earlier in the evening. *What the hell just happened?* If she were a fanciful person at all, Sunnie might believe she'd stepped into an alternate universe. One where her two best friends weren't off-limits and the attraction she'd fought against for years was returned.

2

RAND WATCHED Sunnie struggle to comprehend what had happened between her and Z. He'd been fairly sure she'd noticed his own arousal earlier, but she didn't bring it up so neither did he. Now though, they were all going to have to deal with the electricity currently arcing between them.

Years ago he and Z had made a pact—Sunshine Michaels was off limits. It had always struck him as funny that they'd been zapped by the *sun* at the exact same moment. He could recall the afternoon as though it had happened only hours ago.

It was the end of year school picnic and the girls were all stretched out on towels baking their oil-slicked limbs under the harsh summer sun. Except Sunnie. She was right in the middle of the football game the boys had started. Unconcerned with her near-naked state, she'd flung herself into one tackle after another until she got her hands on the ball. Taking off on those mile-long legs, she'd dodged and weaved between players. When she broke clear of their defense line, he and Z had been the only two fast enough to catch her.

Sand kicked up behind her and in spite of the clingy, shifting grains beneath his feet Rand caught up, but as he reached out to grab her she darted to the side. If it wasn't for Z being a step behind him she'd have been clear. Instead, the three of them collided in a bone-crunching impact that took them to the ground in a tangled heap. Sunnie ended up pinned beneath them and for the first time in his life Rand discovered one of his best friends was a girl.

A *stacked* girl.

He'd looked at Z and found the same discovery swirling in his friend's eyes. At that point Sunnie started a yelling match that had them both scrambling to their feet, but the damage was done. Neither of them ever looked at her the same way again. And regardless of their newly discovered mutual desire, they managed to not only remain friends with each other, but strengthen the friendship between all three of them. Through university, boyfriends, girlfriends, shitty jobs, great jobs, you name it, they'd experienced it all and stuck together.

For years they'd kept their true feelings for Sunnie hidden. Until now. In the space of a few hours something had shifted, some indefinable atom of the world had moved and Rand hadn't a clue what or how. All he knew was it started when she arrived home early from another bad date.

"Your date."

"What?" Sunnie turned to face him. "My date?"

"What was wrong with him?"

"Um...nothing a crowbar wouldn't fix."

"A crowbar?" What the hell was she talking about?

"To pry the third wheel off."

"Huh?" Rand shook his head. "Could you not speak in riddles?"

Sunnie took a deep breath, one that raised her chest and

pushed her breasts out. He couldn't stop his gaze from dipping to the deep cleavage her tight dress gave her, but her whole body appeared to deflate as she let the breath go and leaned back against the couch, her eyelids lowering.

"He brought someone with him."

"What?" Rand's hands clenched into fists and anger churned his gut. "He two-timed you on your date?"

"No, apparently it was supposed to be a three-person date."

"What the fuck?" Was she saying what he thought? "He brought a friend with him?" Rand knew he wasn't getting it. At least he hoped he wasn't getting it.

"Not a friend."

"Sunshine, you're not being clear. Did he bring someone with him or not?"

"Yeah." Her throat work as she swallowed. "His wife."

Dumbfounded, Rand sat staring at Sunnie's profile. Her eyes were closed and her lips were drawn down at the end. Before he could form a coherent thought, never mind speak, she turned her head and opened her eyes.

"Why do I always attract the rotten ones?"

Rand's heart ached. "Aw, Sunshine, attracting rotten ones isn't your problem. It's more that you attract *all* types, but you don't seem to notice the ones that aren't aggressive in their pursuit. How many times did this guy ask you out before you agreed?"

"At least once a week for the last few months."

"And why did you finally agree to go out with him?"

Sunnie ducked her head, her neck and cheeks flushing pink. "To shut him up."

"Thought so." Rand placed two fingers under her chin and nudged her head back so she had to look at him. "You're not picking these guys, Sunnie. You're giving in to the ones that won't take no for an answer. The fact they won't accept no should tell you something."

"So it's not me, it's them?"

Her hopeful look made Rand want to pull her close and agree, but he couldn't deceive her. "No, Sunshine, it *is* you. You need to open your eyes and look at what's around you. There are so many decent guys that would jump at the chance to be with you."

"Really?"

Rand could no more stop his hand from cupping her cheek than he could stop breathing. The action was involuntary, one that felt so natural and so right that the next move was to lean in and kiss her slightly parted lips. He brushed Sunnie's mouth with his. Pressed against that soft, warm flesh with growing eagerness and took them both onto shaky ground. The world shifted—a single jolt that rocked Rand to his toes and delivered a breath-stealing fist to his gut.

He pulled back, his eyes opening slowly. When had they closed? Sunnie blinked, confusion and desire swirling in the depths of her baby blues. Emotions Rand understood all too well. That kiss, nothing more than a brush of lips, had exploded in a way he never imagined. The desire he'd held tight rein of all his adult life had gotten a taste of forbidden fruit. How was he supposed to deny himself now?

"Rand?"

His name tripped off her lips on a soft breath, and warm air flowed over his face. He shuddered. The teasing caress along with her sultry voice stirred his lust further, pumped hot blood through his veins and into his groin. He'd never heard her speak in that tone before. Never dreamed he would. Knowing he'd been the one to make her breathless with such a simple kiss had Rand wondering what he could do with a full seduction.

Would her breath hitch when he stroked her skin? Catch when he pressed his erection against her?

She searched his eyes, but he couldn't find the words to reassure her. Wasn't sure they existed. Not now. Nothing could return them to the way they were before that kiss. Their gazes remained locked, their mouths a few inches apart, and Rand wanted to move in and plant his lips on hers again. He needed to put distance between them or that's exactly what would happen. Leaning back, he moved a few inches away, managed to give his cock a little room in his pants as well as widen the gap separating their bodies.

"Why...?" She brought her hand up and covered her lips with trembling fingers. "You kissed me. Like you *wanted* to."

Rand laughed. "Don't sound so surprised, Sunshine. I want to do a hell of a lot more than kiss you."

"R-really?"

Her disbelief made him laugh harder. "Shit, Sunnie, you have no idea how much."

She studied him a moment before glancing over her shoulder at the door where he could hear Z in the other room talking on the phone. Her gaze returned to meet Rand's. "What about Zeke?"

"Oh I'm pretty sure he'd give his left nut to go well beyond a kiss."

"Who's giving up a nut and to whom?" Z asked as he rejoined them.

"You are, for more than a kiss with Sunnie." Rand watched Sunnie's cheeks turn a deeper red.

"No shit, Sherlock. She can have both, and any other body part she's interested in for that matter." Z sat on the other side of Sunnie, sandwiching her between them.

An image of Sunnie, wedged between him and Z, flickered across Rand's mind. He dragged in a deep breath. Where the image came from he didn't know, but he liked every delicious second of it. He'd watched numerous porn movies in his life but never imagined Sunnie, Z and himself in the starring roles. The more he thought about it, the more he wanted it with a bone-deep urgency he struggled to control. Maybe that would be the solution to all their problems—a way around the pact.

"What are you thinking, Rand?" Z eyed him from the other end of the couch.

"How well the three of us fit together." He swallowed hard, took a breath and went for it. "How well that would translate to sex."

Beer sprayed from Sunnie's mouth. "*Sex?*" She broke into a fit of coughing.

"Oh man." Z thumped Sunnie's back, a grin spreading on his face. "Didn't see that one coming. I'm flattered, man. Didn't know you thought of me in that way. But I have to admit, I'm intrigued."

"You are?" Sunnie squeaked as she tried to catch her breath.

"Relax, Sunshine, we're not going to pounce on you." Rand rubbed his hand up and down her spine. "It's not like either of us hasn't thought about having sex with you before now."

"Ha-ha, as if." Her gaze switched between them.

"Every damn day since our high school end of year picnic," Z said.

Rand nodded. "Yep, best and worst day of my life."

"Yeah, I'm with you on that, man."

"What?" Sunnie jumped up and turned to face them. "You're not making any sense. What has this got to do with high school?"

"We've both wanted to get in your pants since then." Rand shrugged, hoping his blunt confession wouldn't send her running for the hills.

"But you never said anything." She began to pace. "Either of you." More pacing. "Ever."

"We made a pact not to," Z said.

Sunnie stopped and spun around, hands on her hips. "What? A pact? Jesus, is this one of those male bonding thingies?"

Rand cracked up. "You say that like you're chewing on dirt."

"Besides, it was nothing so elaborate. We discussed it at the time, and decided we valued our friendship more than having sex with you."

She looked at Z. "I'm surprised either of you were mature enough to come up with that idea."

"Hey!" Rand went to stand but she stopped him with a hard stare and a pointed finger.

"I remember what hound dogs you both were in high school and at university. Anything in a skirt was fair game."

"Defense mechanism." Z's cryptic comment had them both turning to look at him.

"What?"

"Huh?"

"When you can't have what you want, surround yourself with what you can. And you know as well as we do that every one of those women were more than happy to be on the receiving end of attention from either one of us." Z reached out and grabbed Sunnie's wrist. "Don't turn the conversation away from what Rand brought up."

Damn. Z was right. She'd used their past behavior to change the topic. Rand couldn't blame her. They were all treading on some dangerous ground. He figured the best thing to do now would be to let it lie for a while. Let Sunnie stew on it for a few days before bringing it up again.

"Look, forget I said anything. Let's just watch the movie

and enjoy a couple of beers." He stood up and stretched. "I'll grab us all a refill. Z, you clear away the boxes."

"But..." Sunnie stood still as they moved around her.

"Relax, Sunshine. It's just three friends spending Friday night watching some daggy old movie," Rand said.

Rand collected their empties and Sunnie's half full one. He left the room with Z right behind him. Neither of them spoke until they were in the kitchen, out of Sunnie's hearing.

They spoke in unison.

"What brought that on?"

"I kissed her."

There was a heartbeat of silence.

"Wait. You kissed Sunnie? When?" Z asked.

"When you left the room to take your call."

"Why?"

"Why?" Rand shook his head as he tipped the rest of Sunnie's beer down the sink. "I can't believe you asked that. I don't know how it happened. One second we were talking about her crummy date and the next my hand was cupping her face and my mouth was on hers." He tossed the bottles in the recycle bin.

"Good?"

"What do you think?"

"I think it smashed the wall holding you back and that's why you brought up sex. I've been feeling my own wall beginning to crumble recently, too."

"No. The wall—the pact—still stands. I was suggesting a loophole."

"A threesome?"

Rand stared at his best friend in disbelief. "What did you think I was talking about?"

"Sex." Z rubbed a hand over his chin. "Then again, now

that I think about it with a little more blood in my brain, you can't be talking about much else, can you?"

"No."

"Were you serious?"

"About sharing her? Yes." Rand pulled open the fridge and grabbed three beers. "I've never thought about it before tonight. Don't really know why I'm thinking that way now. Other than that strange sharing comment she made earlier, none of us have ever voiced our interest in a physical relationship, but the more the idea circles in my head the more I want to make it happen."

"We're walking on quicksand."

"I know, but I can't say I'm sorry I brought it up." He passed a bottle to Z.

"Thanks." Z cracked the top open. "What now?"

"Leave it. You know what she's like. She'll mull it over for a while before she decides anything."

"Yeah, but she's never dated anyone who hasn't badgered her into it. You think this will be different?"

Rand thought about it for a moment. "Yeah, I do."

"Why?" Z asked. "How can you be sure she won't just forget about it like every other guy who's asked her out once?"

"Because *we're* different."

Z COULDN'T CONCENTRATE on the movie. Not when the conversation with Rand was stuck on continuous replay in his head. As much as he tried he couldn't help but wonder: *were* they different? They'd never treated Sunnie as anything other than a friend and housemate. Even gone out of their way to be sure there was no hint of sexual attraction between them, the risk of complicating—or worse—destroying their friendship always hanging over their heads. He and Rand had always been on the same page where Sunnie was concerned.

Nothing and no one should be allowed to hurt her—including them.

For as long as he'd known her, one thing had been crystal clear. Sunnie wanted the whole *happy ever after* deal, complete with Prince Charming, white picket fence and two kids, preferably a boy and girl. He couldn't blame her. No child grew up with three fathers and an indifferent mother without scars, and Sunnie's were in her obsession to be normal. But over the years Sunnie had proven her propensity for dating assholes—as if she subconsciously chose them on purpose. Her mother's eccentric life and sporadic interest had scarred Sunnie deeply, and Z often got the impression Sunnie felt herself unworthy of love.

It wasn't until he'd taken a psychology class at university that he really began to understand what motivated her. She never dated anyone who didn't put in a huge effort to gain her attention only to turn the tables and suffocate the guy once she accepted his interest. Z couldn't count the number of times he and Rand had propped her up after another loser had broken her heart.

Or more accurately, shattered her dream of falling in love and living the perfect life.

With Sunnie's unusual parentage you would expect her to be more unconventional in her attitude, but she never did anything that could be considered risqué. She almost hadn't moved in with them because sharing a house with two guys bordered on out of the ordinary in her eyes. He smiled at the memory. It had taken weeks to talk her into it. Weeks of bribing and begging, but finally she'd caved. Of course it had helped that her flatmate at the time had moved out and Sunnie couldn't afford the rent on their inner-city apartment on her own. And it didn't hurt that they promised to let her redecorate the place.

In five years there hadn't been a serious argument between

them. The occasional squabble over who left the wet towel on the bathroom floor didn't count. Except there was that small thing of them taking advantage of her. When the last woman Rand had broken up with had pointed out neither of them needed a woman when they already had a *wife* in such a nasty way, Z had at first taken offense, but then he'd really thought about it and hadn't liked what he'd discovered about the way he treated Sunnie at all.

Weeks of mulling over the issue had brought him to the conclusion that he needed to not only pull his weight around the house, but also do things for Sunnie like she did for him. Rand had agreed with him when Z had brought the subject up and, rather than say anything to Sunnie, they simply became better housemates. Of course Sunnie knew them too well and smelled a rat. At least she hadn't dug too deep into the reason for the change. She didn't need to know the full details of Melody's accusations. Staring sightlessly at the television, Z swallowed the last of his beer.

"Anyone want another one?" he asked as he got to his feet.

"Sure. I'm almost done." Rand tipped his bottle to his mouth.

Z looked at Sunnie and tried not to laugh, but he was fighting a losing battle. She'd fallen asleep, her head at a weird angle and the beer in her hand in danger of spilling in her lap. He reached over and plucked the bottle from her hand. She didn't stir.

"She's out cold," he said.

Rand glanced over at her. "I knew I shouldn't have let her open that last one."

"Oh come on, she hasn't had that many." Z placed his and Sunnie's bottles on the table.

"Four is too many for Sunnie and you know it." Rand stood. "Better get her into bed."

"I'll do it. You took care of her last time."

"That's because you were just as shit-faced."

"Hey, we were celebrating." Z recalled they'd polished off a whole bottle of tequila that night.

"Dumping your latest bimbo isn't cause for celebration, Z."

"It most certainly is when the woman was out picking rings without my knowledge." He leaned over to slide one arm under Sunnie's legs and the other under her shoulders. "Escaping hell is always worth a party."

Rand laughed. "You weren't thinking that way before she went jewelry shopping."

Z shrugged. "What can I say? She was good in the sack."

Sunnie mumbled as he lifted her off the couch. He shushed her with nonsense words whispered into her hair. Z nodded in the direction of her room and waited for Rand to go first. Careful not to bash her head or feet into any walls, he followed his friend down the hall to Sunnie's room. After Rand pulled back the quilt on her perfectly made bed, Z placed her on the clean sheet.

"Should we take her dress off?" Rand asked. It wouldn't be the first time they'd stripped a drunk Sunnie of her clothes and put her to bed, but after their earlier conversation Z didn't think it'd go down too well with her this time.

"You want to explain in the morning if we do?"

"Ah, no. Guess we'll just cover her up then."

"Yep." Z grabbed the bedding and gently covered Sunnie.

"Still up for another beer?" Rand asked as they walked out of the room.

"Sure." Z glanced at his watch and laughed. "It's not even ten o'clock."

"I know. That's our Sunshine, the last of the party animals." Rand headed for the kitchen. "Are you really going to drag her out of bed in the morning?" he asked as he pulled two beers from the fridge.

"She agreed to come with us." Z took the beer his mate offered.

"Yeah, but she was onto the fourth beer by then."

"A promise is a promise," Z said with a smile as he walked to the lounge room.

"Shit. I hope the waves are good 'cause she's gonna kill us."

"By the time she's awake enough to do that we'll be in the water far out of reach." He cracked the top on his beer and took a swig.

"I bags not getting her up then."

"Fine, you load the boards in my truck and I'll drag Sunshine out of bed." Z propped his feet up on the coffee table. "What time do you want to leave?"

"Sunrise is five thirty-nine. If we leave here at five we'll be in the water by five thirty."

"What's the swell?"

"Four foot." Rand took a sip of his beer. "But that's only if the storm moving up the coast continues at the same speed. If the winds pick up we'll get about six before the bad weather hits."

"Nice either way." Z took another mouthful of beer. "So, Sunnie."

"Mm, what about her?"

"We're going to do this?"

"If it's what she wants." Rand tapped the bottle against his chin. "I still think we should let her stew on it a few days, possibly even weeks before mentioning it again."

"I don't think we should wait that long. Don't get me wrong. I don't think we should push it either, but I think we need to keep it at the forefront of her mind."

"We are not going to be like all those SOBs that couldn't take no for an answer," Rand said.

"No, we're not. But we're also not going to be like all those saps that got knocked back once and tucked tail."

"It's a fine line."

Z grinned. "Yeah, but we've both got excellent balance."

Rand laughed. "That we do, that we do."

"It probably helps that we've both got thick heads too."

Rand looked at him. "Why?"

"So it won't hurt as much when she bashes them together."

3

THE SUN, barely over the horizon, lacked heat but Sunnie had no doubt it would be a regular summer scorcher before midday. Luckily she'd be long gone before it got too hot or the crowds arrived to fill Sydney's most famous beach. She couldn't believe Rand and Z had talked her into joining them for their early morning surf. Not that she planned to catch any waves— she'd leave that to them—she was more than happy to lie back on her towel and enjoy the sight of all the die-hard surfers riding the waves in their clingy board shorts and bare chests. Not to mention Bondi's yummy surf lifesavers.

"Hey stranger."

Lifting her eyelids Sunnie glanced up the beach and saw her friend Piper coming toward her. "Hey, been a while."

"It has. And imagine my surprise to find you gracing the sand this early in the day." Piper spread her towel out beside Sunnie and sprawled on top.

Sunnie grinned. "Yeah, I know. But they caught me at a weak moment."

Piper glanced her way, one delicate eyebrow arched.

"Rand and Z took advantage of my drunken state last night."

Her friend sat bolt upright. "Really?" Pip's smile spread from ear to ear, almost splitting her face in two. "Do tell."

Sunnie laughed and pushed herself up to sit. "Not that kind of advantage."

Piper sighed. "Shame. Getting caught between those two would be…" She shuddered.

"Piper!"

"What?"

"You're living with not one, but two gorgeous guys, and you're thinking of Rand and Z that way."

Piper laughed. "Don't worry, it's my boys I'm picturing not yours." She eyed Sunnie. "You know I can't believe you've never thought of going there."

Sunnie turned to look at the shore. "They're not *mine*. They're my best friends. I've never thought about them that way before."

"Before?" Piper asked.

"You know what I mean."

"No, no, I don't think I do. There was something different in the tone of your voice this time. Every other time you've used the *best friends* protest I believed you." Pip placed her hand on Sunnie's arm. "What gives, Sunnie?"

With a sigh, Sunnie pulled her knees up and wrapped her arms around her shins. Staring at the waves rolling in, she tried to figure out what to say.

"Did something happen?" Piper asked.

"No. Yes. But not what you're thinking or hoping for." Sunnie tried to sort her thoughts into order. "Let's see. My date was a rat bastard. Rand checked out my boobs and got a boner when he hugged me. I nearly kissed Z. Rand kissed me then suggested we'd all click when it came to sex. They finally both admitted to wanting to get in my pants since high school."

"Whoa. Wait. Slow the fuck down." Piper shook her head. "Let's start with the perving and boner. We'll ignore the rat bastard. They're never worth rehashing."

"You said it. But then it was the rehashing of the rat bastard that led to the other two."

"Interesting segue."

Sunnie shrugged. "Not really. I was wearing a dress that emphasized the girls, so the perving was more a guy reflex I think. And the boner came when Rand tried to stop me from crying over my disastrous love life."

"The only disaster is your choice in dates, Sunnie. You're looking everywhere but right under your nose. But let's get back to the good stuff." Piper leaned closer. "What happened with the almost-kiss with Z?"

"I don't know how to explain it. There was this charged moment and I realized I wanted to kiss him."

"How'd you get to the *charged moment*?"

"We were wrestling for the TV remote."

"Ah, body contact. What about the actual kiss with Rand?"

"That came later. We were talking one minute and then he was kissing me. It was over before it really started, but..."

"But what?"

"I don't know." Sunnie shrugged. "I don't understand any of it."

"So how did the subject of sex come up? That's a big leap from a quick kiss to sex."

"Again I'm at a loss. I can't seem to get my head around it, never mind explain it to you."

"Okay, let's try it this way. How did the kiss make you feel?"

Sunnie tried to remember all the emotions that had churned inside her after Rand's kiss. "Disappointed. Aroused. Scared."

"And the idea of the three of you having sex?"

One thing Sunnie had always admired about Piper was her honesty and fearlessness. She just wished she had a smidgen of either—she might not feel so uncomfortable talking about last night if she did. Then again, it all came down to choices, didn't it? If she chose to be honest and brave, she would be. "Terrified and excited."

"But not disgusted?"

"What?" Sunnie whipped her gaze away from the water to meet Piper's. "No. Never. God. I have thought of them and sex before. Shit, you'd have to be dead not to notice how hot they are. But I've never gone there for more than a second. And I've never thought of them...together."

Once she started Sunnie couldn't stop the flow of words.

"I've wished on more than one occasion that I could fall for one of them, but they're my best friends. I can't think of one without the other, so how could I ever choose between them?"

"Who said you have to choose one over the other?"

Sunnie laughed, a sharp bark of sound that held no real mirth. "Piper, living in a three-way relationship may work for you, but it's definitely not the norm."

"Neither was being gay a few years ago. Now look how far the world has come."

Mouth gaping, Sunnie stared at her friend.

"Oh come on, do you really think we'd be where we are today if everyone followed what was acceptable? Think of all those explorers who sailed off in search of new lands that others said didn't exist. And what about the astronauts determined to walk on the moon." Piper placed her hand on Sunnie's shoulder and gave a gentle squeeze. "The sky's the limit and the sky is endless, Sunnie."

"But—"

"No buts. Go for what you want."

"I don't know what I want," Sunnie moaned.

Piper pulled her into a brief hug. "Yes you do. You just have to be honest and admit it."

"I've spent my whole life trying to live down my parents and the whole three-fathers-one-mother thing. Done everything, including changing my name, to be normal, and now I'm going to throw all that away by pursuing my two best friends." Sunnie pulled her knees tighter against her chest and rested her forehead on top. "God. I just basically admitted I want to do this."

Piper chuckled and patted Sunnie's back. "Yes you did, and you can bet your next paycheck I'm not going to let you forget it."

"Some friend you are."

"Let's see if you still feel that way after the dust settles."

Sunnie lifted her head and laid her chin on her knees. She watched as Rand and Z waded out of the surf. Their bodies glistened in the morning light, their leg muscles flexing with each step. Rand's height and bigger build moved with purpose, while Z's slightly smaller frame had a relaxed, almost lazy motion. Warmth pooled in her lower belly, her nipples hardened, and her sex clenched. Damn. Now that she'd let herself think about them in a sexual way her body was raring to go. Taking a shuddering breath, she turned to Piper.

"So what do I do now?"

"I can't tell you that. I *can* tell you that if it's meant to happen it will if you're open to it."

"Isn't there some sort of order? Some game plan I should follow?"

Laughing, Piper shook her head. "This isn't the *norm*, remember? No pre-trod steps for you to follow, I'm afraid. And really, would you want to do this someone else's way?"

"No." Sunnie didn't need to think about it. If she was going to take this new twist in her friendship with Rand and Z any further then it would be on her terms. Their terms. Her eyes were drawn back to the two men slowly making their way across the sand. "No, it would have to be our way."

FROM THE CORNER of his eye, Z peeked at Sunnie as he strode through the shallows. She'd not been a happy camper when he woke her before dawn, but he wasn't about to give her the chance to sneak out of the house while they were catching some morning waves. And he was pretty sure that's exactly what she would do if they weren't back when she finally rolled out of bed. He'd thought about disabling her car but last time he'd done that Sunnie had made his life a living hell for three straight weeks. He smiled. One thing he could always count on was her passion for whatever she had on her mind. She did everything with one hundred and ten percent.

His cock stirred. He could only imagine what it would be like to have that dedication aimed at him in bed. A shiver snaked down his spine. Christ, what he wouldn't give for a little of her amorous attentions. Blood pounded in his groin and filled his flesh with urgent need. *Crap.* Z shifted his board to hide the throbbing bulge in the front of his shorts. Glancing at Rand, he saw his friend had also pulled his board across his body and Z was reminded of the fact he wasn't the only one interested in Sunnie.

Except Rand had already kissed her—tasted her.

Jealousy churned in Z's stomach and he wanted to snatch Sunnie away from Rand, but the very idea tasted foul on his tongue and heavy in his chest as though he were betraying his best friends. They'd been a trio for so long that even when he'd fantasized about doing Sunnie, Rand had been there in the back of his mind. To him they were inseparable.

"What kind of reception do you think we'll get?" Rand asked.

"Depends on what you're talking about." Z glanced at Rand before moving his gaze to Sunnie and the woman next to her. "If you're referring to getting her out of bed at the crack of dawn then all it'll take is a detour to the drive-through for her favorite morning feast. If, on the other hand, you're referring to the suggestion of us taking our little threesome into the bedroom, I haven't a clue, but I do know I'm not about to let it drop."

"No?"

"Hell no." Z lifted his chin in Sunnie's direction. "She's the one thing I've always wanted and could never have. Not without you, anyway."

Rand sighed. "It's weird, but I understand that sentiment completely."

"I should probably make it clear now that any sex between the three of us would be about her. I love you, man, but not that way."

Laughter burst from Rand's lips. "I hear ya. I swear, I was just trying to work out how to say that very thing."

Z smiled. "At least we're on the same page there."

"Yeah, but what page are we on and where do we go from here?"

"I haven't got a clue. Guess we turn the next page." Z shrugged. "I've never done this before."

"And you think I have?"

"No." Z stopped and turned to face his friend. "Shit, Rand, that's not what I meant. I'm saying I'm as clueless as you are."

"I guess we play it by ear, wait to see what happens."

"Oh no, I'm not waiting. I plan to launch an all-out seduction. But first we have to face the fire over dragging her ass out of bed this morning." Z started in Sunnie's direction again. "Oh, and cancel any plans you have for the weekend. I've got an idea starting to take shape. Just need to make a phone call when we get home."

"Care to enlighten me?"

"Not yet." They'd almost reached where Sunnie sat on her towel. "Besides, I don't want to give Sunnie a chance to protest."

"Protest what?" Sunnie asked from a few feet away.

Damn. "Being dragged out of bed before your namesake, what else?" He hoped her grumpiness over this morning was enough to distract her.

"I was just saying how surprised I was to see Sunnie this early," Piper said. "But then, I can just imagine how persuasive you two can be."

"I'll take that as a compliment." Z bent down and laid his board on the sand before grabbing his towel. "Where's Sam and Nate?"

"Out there." Piper pointed over Rand's shoulder. "They got here later than usual."

The grin on Piper's face and the little shudder that sent her breasts jiggling, drawing his attention to her hard nipples beneath her top, hinted at why her housemates had been late. Z decided to stir her up a little. "Can't think of anything that would keep me from my morning surf."

Piper's cheeks flushed red but he didn't think it had anything to do with the rising sun. "You obviously haven't had the right incentive to stay in bed then."

He smiled. "I'm pretty sure there's nothing more enticing than the waves at dawn."

Her smile should have clued him in but he wasn't prepared for the visual imagery her comeback delivered.

"Oh I'm pretty sure you'd be happy to stay in bed if you had a naked Sunni beside you."

"Piper!" Sunnie cried.

Rand half laughed, half choked beside him. With a naked Sunnie stretched out in his imagination Z couldn't think of a response. His brain had bled out in an effort to supply his cock.

"Cat got your tongue, Z?" Piper smirked.

"Damn woman. You've never struck me as the in-your-face type," Rand said as he shook his head. "Then again, you are living with two guys."

"That's not all I'm doing with them." Piper waggled her eyebrows suggestively, making Rand laugh.

Z's mouth opened. Closed. Opened. Words refused to form on his tongue. She'd always come across as shy and businesslike. Obviously he didn't know the woman his two friends were living with very well at all.

Piper laughed and clutched her sides. "You should...see the...look on...your face."

"I think that's our cue to go." Sunnie stood. "I'm starving and you two owe me breakfast."

"Aw, spoilsport. It was just getting fun." Piper's words were laced with laughter. "Ring me during the week, Sunnie. Let me know how it goes."

"How what goes?" Rand asked.

"Nothing." Sunnie turned away and quickly gathered her things.

"Her date," Piper added.

"What date? You don't have a date tonight." Z spun around. She couldn't have a date.

"I don't."

"Then what's Piper talking about?" His gaze bounced between the two women. "What date?"

"Calm down, caveman. I'm talking about last night's date." Piper got to her feet and hugged Sunnie, whispering something in her ear that made her blush.

Z couldn't hear what was said, but the idea that Sunnie might be hiding something from him didn't sit well. Piper had every right to call him a caveman because right now he'd like to grab Sunnie by her ponytail and drag her back to the house. The thought of her with another guy made his gut clench and his head pound. How had he survived her dating all these years?

RAND REACHED the supermarket checkout as Z pulled into a parking spot by the front doors. He could see Sunnie through the windshield already chomping into a breakfast burger. A smile played at the edges of his mouth until he realized the cashier thought he was aiming it at her. As fast as possible, he paid for his purchases and left. Holding the door open for an elderly woman slowed him down, but it gave him time to enjoy the view. Nothing made him feel as good as seeing Sunnie happy, and right now he'd say she bordered on ecstatic.

She took another bite and dropped her head back against the seat. Her eyes closed and her jaw moved slowly as she savored her mouthful before swallowing. The urge to kiss those smiling lips sliced into him, cramping his gut and stealing his breath. Walking over, he yanked her door open and leaned in. His mouth found hers just as her tongue flicked out to lick her lips and he took full advantage. Thrusting his tongue into her mouth, he teased hers until she softened under him. Rand took his time, pulled back to coax her into being the aggressor, then changed his mind and dived deep again.

He swallowed the moan that slipped from her throat, breathed it in and dragged that little piece of her inside to always be his. Rand brought one hand up to cup her head; his fingers tangled around her ponytail and he tightened his grip. With a sharp tug, he tilted her face to join their mouths completely. She moaned again, her lips pliant beneath his. They fought for control, each taking with haste what the other freely gave. A combination of pleasure and pain centered in his groin where his hard-on pressed against the car seat, but that didn't stop him. It was Z's words that ripped him out of his lust haze.

"You two need to stop or I'm coming over there to join in, and that's bound to get us arrested." Z's words were raspy, rough as though he spoke through gravel.

Rand separated his mouth from Sunnie's and studied her through hooded eyes. Her eyelids fluttered open to reveal dilated pupils with a thin blue ring around them. He searched her gaze for anger but all he could find was desire that mirrored his own. With difficulty, he dragged in a breath and moved away. Stepping back, he closed her door and opened the rear one. The lock clicked behind him a second before Z threw the car into gear and reversed out of the spot.

"In a hurry?" he asked.

"Damn straight I am. Do you have any idea what that little show did to me?"

"I have a bit of a clue." Rand raked his fingers through his hair.

He buckled himself into the middle seat, making sure the seat belt didn't dig into his erection, and stared through the front window as Z tore out of the parking lot. The ride home was fast, but thankfully uneventful. Z whipped the truck into the driveway and slammed on the brakes. Rand threw out his hand and braced himself on the front seat.

"Shit, Z, you trying to kill us?" He undid his belt and slid across the bench. His feet hadn't even touched the ground when Z appeared beside Sunnie's door. "Take a breath, man."

"I'm trying, but certain people aren't making it easy for me."

"You just need to take the edge off."

Before Rand could work out what Sunnie meant she leaned out her open door and into Z's arms, her mouth planted on his. Mesmerized by the sight of them kissing, Rand held his breath as their lips and tongues ate at each other. Devoured. He licked his lips, remembering the press of Sunnie's against them. Her taste. The urgent need to feast on her. His cock throbbed to the beat of his racing heart, the engorged flesh beneath his shorts painfully confined. They had to take this inside before it got out of hand.

"Enough." He jumped from the truck. "Inside. Now."

Z and Sunnie sprang apart and Rand quickly gripped Sunnie's elbow, pulling her toward the front door. The truck doors closed behind him and Z's bare feet slapped against the concrete drive as he rushed to catch up. Sunnie kept pace with his long strides but tripped on the bottom step as he took them two at a time. Rand slid his arm around her waist and pulled her in close to keep her from falling.

"Slow down, Rand." She yanked herself from his grasp. "I'm not going anywhere but inside. There's no need to manhandle me."

"Sorry." He stepped aside to let Z pass to unlock the door.

"Don't you want to get your boards?" Sunnie asked.

"Later."

"Rand, I said I wasn't going anywhere. You need to put your boards away."

He glanced at the truck then over at Z. "Dammit. Okay."

Z turned the key and pushed the door open. "Here, we'll get the boards sorted while you finish breakfast."

Rand noticed the bag in Sunnie's hand. The brown paper top crumpled in her fist, the bottom dark with the telltale sign of greasy hash browns. His stomach rumbled. He'd forgotten all about eating. Couldn't even remember what he'd ordered. Shit. He needed to pull it together and stop acting like a boy getting laid for the first time. Where was his control? With Sunnie he didn't seem to have any. One touch and his mind took a vacation.

"Don't eat mine. We'll be five minutes, tops." He jogged down the steps. The quicker they dealt with the boards the quicker he could get his hands on her again.

"No rush. I'll be inside waiting," Sunnie called out behind him.

He reached the back of Z's truck and untied the boards.

"Either it's been too long since I had sex or the chemistry between us is off the scale. I'm so close to blowing the front of my shorts are wet and it isn't sea water," Z said as he joined Rand.

"Tell me about it." Rand glanced at his friend as he slipped a hand down to adjust himself. "And for the record it's been months for me but I took care of business last night in the shower. Should have known then it would be explosive once we did touch her."

"And we haven't gotten to the good stuff yet." Z lifted his board from the truck and walked over to the side of the house. "Hurry up, man. For someone that was keen to forget about our boards you sure are taking your sweet time."

Rand gave Z the bird and got a face full of water from the hose for his trouble. Spluttering, he ducked behind his board to avoid the next volley of spray. "Knock it off. Sunnie will kill us if we traipse water through the house."

"What's this *we* shit? I'm not wet." Z's words were almost drowned out by the blast that slammed into the other side of Rand's board.

"Shit, Zeke."

"Pansy."

"I'd rather be a pansy than dead which is exactly what Sunnie would make me if you managed to soak me."

"Don't worry. I'm not about to jeopardize Sunnie's good mood."

Rand waited a second before peeking around his board. Much to his relief Z was directing the hose at his own board on the grass. He approached with caution just in case Z had a surprise attack in mind. To be sure, Rand positioned himself between Z and the tap; that way he could turn off the supply before his friend soaked him. It was a wasted effort. True to his word, Z continued to clean, not even glancing Rand's way.

Z handed over the hose when he was done and Rand made quick work of washing off the sand and salt still clinging to his board. The whole time he worked, Sunnie's words replayed in his head over and over. *I'll be inside waiting*. The idea of her waiting thrilled him and his mind kept imagining all kinds of ways she could be preparing for their arrival. His cock strained against his shorts as his blood pumped hard and fast with his escalating arousal. He dropped the hose on the grass and leaned over to turn off the tap.

Rand scooped up the towel Z had tossed on the ground and quickly dried the fiberglass surface. With his board clean and dry he made his way to the open garage door. Z already had his board put away and Rand lifted his into the rack beside it. Once his board was secure he reached down and rearranged his erection in an attempt to alleviate some of the throbbing in his groin. He hoped the prolonged hard-on wouldn't mean he'd go off too soon. He planned to take his time. Explore every little millimeter of Sunnie's skin before finally sinking his length deep in her pussy.

And the strange thing was he wanted to share every moment with Z.

4

SUNNIE CLOSED the door behind her and slumped against it. Her heart raced and her lungs gasped for air in an attempt to keep up. Rand had kissed her. Again. She'd kissed Z. And they were planning to do a whole lot more. A shiver rolled from her head to her toes, raising the hair on her arms and leaving goose bumps in its wake. Nervous excitement buzzed from one nerve ending to another until every part of her vibrated with anticipation. She had no idea how this would turn out. What they expected. What *she* expected. The only thing she did know for sure was there was no going back now.

She'd made up her mind to go for it and she would, but that didn't stop the fear from sneaking in. Her stomach dipped and her throat closed. What if she screwed this up? What if this destroyed the best friendship she'd ever had? Sunnie didn't know what scared her more—the thought of this blowing up in their faces or the idea that a deeper relationship between them would work. Whichever way it went there was no stopping it now. Any second, the guys would come inside and she didn't want them to find her cowering against the door.

Straightening up, she used the timber beneath her shoulder blades to propel herself in the direction of the kitchen. There was no point stressing over the outcome before the event. As her mother always told her—trouble always finds its way into your life; no point borrowing more. And if anyone knew about trouble it was Sunnie's mother. She frowned as memories resurfaced. Giving herself a mental shake, she shoved them all back into the dark corner of her mind where her childhood resided. Last thing she wanted was to revisit that time of her life.

Dumping the greasy takeout bag on the counter, Sunnie pulled out the uneaten food and tossed the sack in the trash. Rand's burger and hash browns were cold so she slipped them onto a plate and into the microwave. The food wasn't the only thing heating up. After Rand's kiss, Sunnie's body temperature had soared and stayed there. Her throat was dry, her skin damp, and the warmth swirling in her belly drew her attention to the moisture pooling between her legs. Embarrassment made her squirm, made muscles tense, but clenching her thighs increased the hum in her sex and sent her internal thermostat off the chart.

She needed to cool down. Opening the fridge, she fanned herself with the cool air but only succeeded in stimulating her sensitized nerves further. Her nipples hardened beneath her top and, with a shudder, Sunnie reached for a Coke and brought the cold can to her face. Goose bumps skipped over her skin as the wet metal made contact with her heated flesh. A shiver raced down her spine. She closed her eyes and attempted to gain control of her senses. The microwave beeped, the front door slammed, and Sunnie knew she was out of time.

Sunnie couldn't let them see her like this. Couldn't let them think she was freaked out by the shift in their relationship. Rand and Z would never follow through if they thought she wasn't one hundred percent on board. Thinking fast, she opened the dishwasher and began unloading the clean dishes. Her fingers trembled as she lifted plates from the rack. Gripping the ceramic tighter only seemed to exaggerate the tremors. The room filled with the sound of rattling dishes and Sunnie didn't hear Z approach until his hand slid over hers where she clutched the crockery so hard her knuckles were white.

"Relax, Sunshine." His breath fanned over the side of her neck and jaw as he leaned in. "We're not doing anything you don't want to."

Rand stepped up beside them and slipped the plates from her grasp. He put them in the cupboard and turned back to her, placing his knuckle under her chin he raised her face until her gaze met his. "If this isn't what you want, Sunnie, say so."

She licked her lips and swallowed past the lump in her throat. "It's not that I don't want to…"

The air around them stilled, as though the room held its breath waiting for her to finish.

"Then why are you shaking?" Z moved closer, his front brushing her back as his arm wrapped around her waist, comforting her.

Rand cupped her face in both hands. "Be honest, Sunshine. If this is going to work there can't be any secrets."

Sunnie knew that, but was reluctant to voice her fears. If she said them aloud, wouldn't that make them real? *Jesus, they're already real.* With a sigh she leaned back against Z's chest. "What if this fucks everything up?"

"We won't let it," Rand said.

"You can't know that."

"Yes. I can." His thumbs made sweeping motions back and forth across her cheeks. "I'll fight tooth and nail for this. For us. If it's what you want."

Rand bent forward and brushed his lips over hers. Her eyelids drifted closed as she savored his touch. But the soft caress of warm flesh didn't last long enough. All too soon, Rand pulled away.

"No." The word left her lips as a breathless plea.

"No, this isn't what you want, or no don't stop?" Z whispered in her ear. His hot breath bathed the sensitive skin on her neck and sent tingles skittering over her jaw.

Rand nibbled on her chin, his open lips pressing on her as his teeth lightly grazed. Z tongued her earlobe before he drew it into his mouth and sucked hard. A puff of air escaped her as she shuddered against them. Rand moved back toward her mouth in a trail of gentle kisses designed to seduce her into following wherever he might lead. It was too much. Not enough.

"More."

Z tugged her ear and sank his teeth into the tender flesh. The sharp sting made her gasp, but a sigh followed when he soothed the pain with a soft lap of his tongue. A moan broke in her throat and when she opened her lips to set it free Rand thrust his tongue into her mouth with greed. He took without restraint. Bold strokes touching and teasing until she had no option but to join in. With a strong demand of her own, Sunnie kissed him back. All the while Z continued to torment her ear and neck.

Sunnie angled her head to seal her mouth to Rand's completely and to give Z more room to move. He didn't disappoint. While she and Rand kissed each other with frenzied need, Z turned his attention to the corded muscle between her neck and shoulder. Treating the area to the same biting and licking he'd lavished on her ear, he sent hot darts of lust careening through her bloodstream to pool in her breasts and pussy. She felt heavy—full—on the verge of bursting and, tearing her mouth from Rand's, she cried out in pleasure.

"Are you sure, Sunnie?" Rand nipped at her lips, moved over her cheek.

Yes. God yes.

"Sunnie?" Z sank his teeth into the rounded edge of her shoulder.

She gasped.

"Answer him."

"Y-yes."

Sunnie felt both their mouths curve into smiles, her skin so sensitized the slightest movement sent waves of desire rolling through her. With each stuttering breath her need grew. Tangling her fingers in Rand's shirt, she pulled him closer, the hot press of his chest on her taut nipples drawing another cry from her.

"Easy, Sunshine," Z murmured against her skin. "We've got all the time in the world."

Z's arm tightened around her waist, his fingers digging into her hip as he pulled her backward. Rand let her go, but Sunnie wasn't about to give him up. She curled her fingers deeper into his shirt and dragged him with them.

"Let him go for a second, Sunnie." Z reached over and tried to pry her fingers loose. He chuckled. "Demanding much?"

Rand laughed as well. "She's always been a stubborn mule when it comes to what she wants. I guess she wants me."

"She can have you, but first I want to get some of her clothes off."

Sunnie let go of Rand's top and grabbed her own. She spun out of Z's hold and yanked the flimsy shirt up her body and over her head, but before she could untangle her arms they caught her between them. Rand snatched the cloth from her grip and proceeded to wrap it around her outstretched forearms. He bound them snugly, not tight enough to cause pain but firm enough to hold her in place.

"What the hell?" She wiggled in an attempt to pull free.

"Uh-uh, no you don't." Rand gave one final tug. "Okay?"

Something stopped her from protesting. The makeshift shackles didn't hurt and Sunnie knew they would free her the second she asked. Plus the swirling warmth low in her belly told her she wasn't opposed to being restrained. Being tied up was new but, as her nipples hardened and her bikini bottoms grew damp, she had to admit it turned her on. Besides, she wanted to see what they had in mind.

"Okay."

"Jesus." Z's curse coincided with his hand covering her breast. "Look at you. Look at the way these babies are on display with your arms like that."

Sunnie glanced down and the movement brought her arms lower.

"No." Rand gripped her wrists in one hand and pulled them back. "Don't move."

Her head was pinned between her arms. It was difficult to tilt her head but she managed to lower her chin and look at what they were doing. Every muscle in her body tightened at what she saw. Z squeezed her right nipple beneath her swim top as Rand flicked at the left with his fingertip. Sunnie moaned. They repeated their actions and a shudder ripped through her. Heavy with arousal, her breasts ached, burned with the need for more.

"Touch me." She arched her spine, thrust her pulsing flesh into their hands.

"We are." Z pinched the taut peak before rubbing the slippery material of her bikini back and forth across the ultrasensitive tip.

"No." Sunnie's knees shook. "Me. Touch *me*."

Rand's hand slid down her outstretched arms until he reached her neck and the bow holding her top up. His nimble fingers dispensed with the knot and the fabric loosened. She cried in frustration when instead of dropping free the material remained between their skin and hers.

"Take it off," she cried.

Z chuckled as he let go of her breast and slid his hand around her ribs to her back. One tug and the remaining strap fell free. Rand curled his fingers, crumpling the thin cloth triangle in his fist. He pulled away and flung the barely there covering over his shoulder. Sunnie didn't have time to moan or gasp as their hands cupped her weighty mounds once more because in the next heartbeat they bent forward and each sucked a nipple into their mouth.

Sunnie's thoughts shattered. Her hips bucked and her pussy clenched as moisture slicked her folds. Rand grazed the puckered flesh with his teeth, flicked at it with his tongue. Z opened his mouth wide and sucked in more of her breast, his tongue lapping at the hard peak. Their touches were different and the contrast drove her mad. It was too much and not enough all at once. She couldn't stop her arms from lowering, the need to hold them to her too great, but the tangled shirt restricted her movements and she couldn't get her hands near them. With a frustrated growl she tugged on the binding, but her efforts were useless; it wouldn't budge.

"Untie me," she pleaded.

In unison they stopped, let go of her breasts and raised their heads to look at her.

"No," Sunnie cried.

Cupping her face, Rand leaned in to brush his lips over hers. "Shh, just relax, Sunshine. Let us do all the work."

"But I want to touch you too."

"If you get your hands on me now it'll be over before it begins. I've waited too long for this moment to have it last only a second," Z said.

"Ditto." Rand's eyes blazed. "In fact I'd like to tie you to my bed. Spread-eagle."

"Oh." The image of herself bound to Rand's bed and at their mercy filled her mind. Her pussy throbbed and she squeezed her legs together.

"You like that idea?" Z asked as he ran his fingertips down her stomach.

She drew in a breath, held it. He watched her closely, never taking his gaze off hers as he toyed with her belly button. Sunnie vibrated with nervous anticipation as she waited—wished—for his hand to go lower. Of their own accord, her hips jerked forward, hinting at what she wanted—needed. Her vision blurred, her chest ached, and Z continued to tease her with his touch.

"Breathe, Sunshine." Rand tapped a finger on the end of her nose. "You're going to pass out if you don't."

Sunnie tried to speak but her lungs had seized, refused to push air in or out. Panic sliced through her. If she collapsed they'd stop. They couldn't stop. She had to draw a breath. Now. Without warning a warm hand cupped her sex. The unexpected touch jolted her body like a live wire. Her chest exploded, the trapped air bursting out on a harsh cry. Arms wrapped around her from behind. When Rand had moved she didn't know, but he held her up, kept her from crumpling to the floor while Z used his hand on her most sensitive spot.

"Fuck. She's burning hot." Z pressed his fingers deeper into her pussy, pushing the soaked material of her bikini between her folds. "She's strung tighter than a bow."

Rand nipped at the side of her neck. "When was the last time you came, Sunnie?"

She couldn't answer, couldn't think about anything but the pleasure Z's actions were giving her. Moaning, she ground her pelvis down on Z's probing hand.

"When, Sunnie?" Rand's teeth tugged on her earlobe.

"Can't. Don't," she panted.

Z leaned over and sucked a nipple into his mouth as his finger circled her clit through her swimmers. Muscles clenched, unclenched, and spasms rolled through her pelvis to center in her womb. She was so close. In two seconds she'd be out of her mind and not remember her own name, never mind when she last got off.

"Want me to tell you when, Sunnie?" Rand's big hand cupped the breast Z wasn't devouring, his fingers brushing over the taut peak.

She moaned. A needy sound that had as much to do with what Rand was saying as what they were doing. Z's mouth found hers, his tongue licking along the seam until she parted her lips and let him in. He pulled back and spoke against her mouth.

"Don't you want to know?" He tugged on her bottom lip with his teeth and Sunnie whimpered as he tweaked the nipple still wet from his mouth.

"I think we should just tell her, Rand." The fingers Z had buried between her legs moved lower; one finger pressed barely inside her through her pants and a shudder shook her.

"Mmm..." Rand murmured against her nape. "I think you're right, Z."

They moved closer, their hard bodies surrounding her in heat. Rand's thick cock snuggled into the crack of her ass while Z's pressed into her hip. Her pussy convulsed in grasping rolls of desperate need. Sensation intensified as they quickened their actions. Sunnie panted, her breathing ragged as she held on by a thin thread.

"The last time you came was..." Rand bit her neck and pinched her nipple hard.

Z thrust his finger deeper and pressed his thumb on her clit. "Now."

God help her, she did. With a raw cry she came apart in their arms. Every bit of her blazed to life, the pleasure so powerful her body lurched and her mind went blank. For long seconds she couldn't breathe—couldn't feel—and then her senses returned tenfold. Her flesh throbbed and pulsed. It was overwhelming. Even the brush of Rand's breath on her neck was too much to take. She squirmed, the slightest touch painful to her inflamed nerve endings.

"Easy now." Rand loosened his hold. "We've got you."

Z pulled his hand from her pussy and smoothed his palm over her hip. "Just breathe, Sunshine. We'll hold you, just breathe."

Her chest heaved with every gasp she dragged in. Pins and needles attacked her hands and feet, and her head spun. She opened her eyes and found Z studying her intently.

"You okay?" he asked.

She gave a slight nod, the only feat she was capable of. Her mouth and throat were too dry to talk but she doubted her brain could manage the command yet anyway. Z cupped her jaw and tilted her head back until she rested against Rand's shoulder. They held her up, but their grip remained light—gentle. With his gaze on hers, Z leaned forward and brushed his lips on her temple. The gesture so soft, so caring, she sighed.

They continued to cradle her as she gradually regained her sanity. She'd never come so hard in her life. Never lost touch with herself long enough to let go that completely. Fatigue gripped her with a vengeance and her eyelids fluttered as she struggled to stay awake. Before she could manage a word, she slipped into an exhausted sleep.

. . .

Z STARED in awed silence at the sleeping form cradled within Rand's arms. Sunnie's breathing was even and a slight smile curled upon her lips. Her skin, damp with a fine sheen of sweat, was flushed pink from head to toe and her nipples stood at attention, topping those generous mounds she called the girls. The air around them was saturated with the scent of her cream and when he glanced down he saw the damp patch on her bikini pants.

"Wow."

"Yeah." Z looked at Rand over Sunnie's head.

"That didn't quite go to plan."

"Didn't know there was one." Z reached down and repositioned his hard-on before his board shorts strangled the thing.

"You mentioned having one earlier." Rand shuffled his feet and got a better grip on the sleeping Sunnie. "We should lay her down."

"Want me to take her?" he asked.

"No. I've got her. Just help me pick her up and I'll carry her to the couch."

Z grabbed Sunnie's hips and supported some of her weight while Rand maneuvered himself so he could slip an arm under her knees. In one smooth motion, his friend scooped her up against his chest.

"The plan?" Rand asked.

"Right, give me a minute to make that call." He reached over and unwound Sunnie's shirt.

"You gonna tell me?"

"I'm checking to see if my brother's beach house is empty. If it is we'll drive up the coast for the rest of the weekend."

"Good idea. It's secluded so there's no chance of someone dropping by unexpectedly and interrupting." Rand turned to take Sunnie to the other room.

Z tossed Sunnie's top through the laundry door and headed

for his bedroom where he'd left his phone this morning. "While she's out we should throw some clothes together and some food. That way we won't have to stop on the way or go out once we're there."

"Okay. You want to pack the food or Sunnie's clothes?" Rand asked as he paused in the hallway.

"I'll grab her stuff, you grab the supplies, but let me check with Gabe first."

He found his phone and scrolled through his contacts until he found Gabriel's name. Hitting Call, Z brought the device to his ear and waited from his brother to pick up.

"Yo, little dude!"

Z's back teeth ground together. He was only one inch shorter than his brother, but Gabriel took every opportunity to remind him of the fact. "G-man."

His brother chuckled. "Get ya every time, man."

In spite of himself, Z smiled. Gabe was the eternal stirrer and he loved nothing more than getting a rise out of his little brother. With a shake of his head, Z got down to business. "Is the beach house empty this weekend?"

"Why? You got some hot babe on the hook you want to shack up with for a few days?"

"Yeah, actually. So can I use the house?"

"Sure, but the hot water is on the fritz so you might be taking cold showers."

Z laughed. "We might *need* those cold showers if this morning is anything to go by."

"Got a live one, have ya? Anyone I know?" Gabe asked.

Z thought about telling his brother but decided against it. The idea of the rest of the world knowing about the step the three of them were taking didn't sit well in his gut. It wasn't that he gave a shit about what anyone might think; more that he wanted to keep their new relationship to himself for a while. "Nah, no one you'd know."

"Fine, keep your secrets. The key is in the usual place."

"Thanks, Gabe."

"No worries, but I'm expecting a full rundown next week sometime."

"We'll see." Z hung up before his brother could protest any further.

"We're going?"

Z turned to find Rand in the doorway. "Yep. Let's get ready. With any luck we can sneak Sunnie into the car and be on our way before she's awake enough to notice."

Rand laughed. "Jeez, do you think we could get that lucky twice in one day?"

"Better pray we do." Z walked over to his dresser and began pulling out a change of clothes. "I've got a feeling she's going to be looking for a hole to fall into once she wakes up and remembers what went on in the kitchen."

"Even so I think we should wake her before we leave."

"Why?" Z threw his clothes on the bed.

"We have to give her choices in this and that includes driving up the coast for the weekend. She may argue against it, but I think we can persuade her to go," Rand said.

"All right." He walked over to his closet and pulled out a sports bag that would fit all their gear in. "But you get to wake the bear."

"Chicken." Rand smiled as he turned away. "Let's get packed first. It'll be harder for her to argue if we're ready to go."

"Now who's chicken?" Z called to Rand's retreating back.

Piling his things in the bag, he headed for Sunnie's room and began going through her drawers. He threw in her sleep shirt and shorts but hoped she wouldn't use them. Rummaging through her clothes he found a pair of swimmers, shorts, and a shirt. At the last second he grabbed sweatpants and sweater just in case the weather cooled off. With everything jammed in the bag Z went to find Rand.

He found him in the living room standing next to a still sleeping Sunnie. There was an icebox on the floor next to the coffee table and a small bundle of clothes folded neatly on top. Z smiled. Rand was such a neat freak when it came to his clothes; his friend would not be pleased when he shoved the carefully folded pile into the sports bag. Grinning, Z dropped the bag on the table and leaned over for Rand's stuff.

"This it?" Z asked.

"Yeah." Rand glanced at him. "Hey, watch it, you'll crease them."

Z laughed. "Who's gonna see? With any luck you won't wear them except for the drive home tomorrow night."

"That may be, but I'd prefer not to look like a homeless hitchhiker you picked up off the street."

"Somehow I don't think a homeless person's budget stretches to brand-name clothing." Z tugged the zipper closed and grabbed the handles. "We going to put these in the car then wake her or you want to wake her first?"

Rand stood still for so long Z thought he might be having a change of heart about the whole thing, but then he spoke. "I'm trying to think like her. Trying to decide which she'd be least pissed at."

Z chuckled. "We've known her for over twenty years and in that time have you *once* been able to predict what would set her off? If you have, you're one up on me."

With a sigh, Rand crouched next to the couch. "Sunnie, time to wake up."

Sunnie slept like the dead mostly and they usually had to shake her awake. Not this time. She bolted upright, the blanket

Rand had covered her with sliding to her waist, revealing her naked torso.

"What? What's wrong?" she grumbled.

Rand casually lifted the covering to her shoulders and held it there. "Nothing, but if you don't get up now you'll sleep the day away."

"Oh." Sunnie blinked several times, her eyes still hazy with sleep.

"Z and I thought it might be nice to head up to Gabe's beach house for the rest of the weekend."

"Um, okay, when will you be back?" she asked in her sleep-roughened voice.

It was obvious Sunnie's mind still hadn't woken entirely because not only did she misunderstand what Rand said but she hadn't realized she was naked from the waist up yet. Z sat on the edge of the coffee table and leaned forward, his elbows resting on his knees.

"What Rand meant was we *all* go up the coast for the rest of the weekend. Kind of like a little vacation."

"Oh." She reached up to brush the hair out of her face and froze. The blanket had dropped on one side, a creamy breast and taut nipple now on display. Sunnie's eyes went wide and her lips parted on a gasp. "Oh!"

Rand scrambled to cover her but Sunnie was trying to get off the couch and wrap the blanket around her at the same time. They ended up in a tangle of arms, legs, and fabric as they toppled to the floor at Z's feet.

"Oh God, oh God, oh God..." Sunnie's whispered mantra was barely heard over the scuffling of the two of them wrestling on the floor.

"Here. Stop." Z bent down and tried to pull the blanket free, but the thing was twisted good and proper around both of them. "Sunnie! Stop moving, dammit."

She stilled long enough for him to get her and Rand separated, but the second she was free she sprang to her feet and ran from the room.

"That went well." Rand lay flat on his back, one hand rubbing his side. "I think she cracked a rib."

Z offered him a hand. "Hey, at least she didn't aim lower." He pulled his friend to his feet. "And I don't think she did it on purpose."

"No, I'd be bleeding if she were serious." Rand glanced at where Sunnie had disappeared. "Now what?"

"I haven't a clue, but I don't think it's wise to let her stew in her embarrassment." Z headed after Sunnie, determined to show her she had nothing to be ashamed of.

5

SUNNIE AVOIDED the mirror above the sink. She knew her face was bright red—she could feel the heat blasting out—there was no need to see it. The curse of having fair skin was the uncontrollable, undisguisable flush of embarrassment that lit her up from head to toe. With a sigh, she sat on the closed toilet lid and dropped her face in her hands. Now that she was completely awake memories of earlier were filling her mind.

Oh my God!

A shiver rolled down her spine and goose bumps broke out on her skin. Her pussy clenched with remembered pleasure and her damp bikini clung to her most intimate places. Sunnie couldn't decide what embarrassed her more, that she'd let them touch her or the abandon with which she'd enjoyed it. And there was no doubt she'd enjoyed every second of their attention, if her explosive orgasm was anything to go by. She'd reveled in their skilled touch.

Sweat covered her whole body, cooling her off to some degree, but the images replaying in her mind continued to raise her temperature. Pushing to her feet, Sunnie reached into the shower and turned on the water just as someone banged on the door making her jump almost clear out of her skin. She spun around but the hinges held. For how long was anyone's guess, from the way they were pounding on the timber panels. It had to be Z. He was the more aggressive of her two friends, although Sunnie had no doubt Rand stood right beside him out in the hall.

"Sunshine, if you don't open this door Z is going to bash it in." Rand's words were muffled by the thick barrier between them and Z's overzealous thumping.

"I'm taking a shower," she called out as she stripped her sticky swimmers off.

Kicking her pants away, Sunnie stepped into the cubicle beneath the warm spray. She ducked her head and let the water rush over her hair and down her back. The gentle flow caressed her skin like a thousand fingers and she shivered in spite of the warmth surrounding her. Sunnie turned and angled so the stream hit the muscles across the top of her back. Her shoulders drooped with relief when the banging stopped only for them to tense up again when she realized what would come next. Sure enough, the door flew open and Z and Rand marched in.

Sunnie wasn't sure what she expected, but a normal conversation certainly wasn't it. She had to hand it to them; after a brief glance down, their gazes returned to her face and stayed there.

"We're packed. If we get on the road in the next thirty minutes we can be at the beach house in time for lunch."

"Umm..." Sunnie couldn't seem to process anything except the fact she was naked and they were standing less than three feet away.

"We'll get back around dinnertime tomorrow. I've got an early morning meeting Monday so I need to be home in plenty of time to get organized," Rand added.

"O-okay."

"Great. We'll pack the car." Z turned to leave. "Oh, I threw your shirt in the wash so you'll need a clean one," he said over his shoulder as he left.

"Want me to pack anything specific for you? Z already threw a change of clothes in the bag for you," Rand said as he gathered up her discarded swimmers and dropped them in the laundry basket.

Sunnie finally managed more than a one-word answer. "No, I'll grab what I want when I get out of the shower."

"We'll wait in the living room then." Rand turned to go but Sunnie stopped him.

"Rand?"

"Yeah?" He kept his back to her.

She wasn't sure what she wanted to say. And until Sunnie got her head around what had taken place before she'd passed out on them, she wouldn't know.

"Do we need to pack food?" she asked instead.

"Done. All you have to do is finish your shower and get dressed. We've taken care of the rest." He strode out of the bathroom, closing the door quietly behind him.

Sunnie stared at the hooks on the back of the door. What the hell just happened? They came in as though she wasn't naked and hadn't shattered in their arms minutes ago. Wait. How long had she been out? She glanced at the frosted glass window above the bathtub but couldn't determine the time of day. It had to be only minutes because Z had talked about getting to Gabe's house for lunch and they'd gotten back from the beach around nine.

Marginally reassured, Sunnie picked up the soap and lathered her hands. She sucked in a breath as her palms skimmed over her sensitive nipples. They hardened beneath the light touch, reminding her again of the episode in the kitchen. Her stomach clenched, her pelvis rocking with the waves of desire pulsing through her pussy. Moaning, Sunnie leaned against the shower wall and dragged her soapy hands lower. The muscles in her belly quivered under her fingertips as she made her way to the throbbing flesh between her legs.

She slid her fingers over her folds, one pressing inside to nudge her clit. The engorged nub, slick to the touch, sent darts of fire into her core. Delving deeper, Sunnie searched out her opening and thrust a finger in to her knuckle while applying pressure to her clit with her thumb. Her legs shook as she pushed herself closer to climax. Leaning more heavily on the tiles behind her, she increased her strokes until her orgasm burst over her like falling rain. A shimmer of pleasure radiated out to every nerve ending, a saturation of lush delight that turned her bones to mush, and she slid down the wall to the wet floor below as a moan of completion tore from her throat.

Her eyes fluttered open to find two burning gazes on her. Caught up in her own pleasure, Sunnie had been oblivious to their return. Rand and Z stood perfectly still except for the harsh breaths their heaving chests dragged in. Their eyes bore holes into her as they stared with barely concealed need. From her position on the floor, Sunnie looked up their bodies affording her a nice view of the large erections tenting their shorts. Without thinking she got to her knees and reached out with both hands to stroke their straining flesh.

They jerked at her touch, their cocks thrusting into her fondling fingers. She cupped their lengths through the material of their board shorts, but it wasn't enough to touch them this way. Sunnie wanted to see them—feel their skin against hers. Her fingers gripped the drawstrings and tugged. In one pull the bows came undone and she quickly yanked on the Velcro zippers to free their erections, but she couldn't manage it one-handed.

"Help me." Sunnie continued to pull on each waistband.

Z moved first. He brushed her hand away and undid his shorts, pushing them past his knees. Rand quickly followed, his shorts and boxers barely over his hips before Sunnie moved back in, her eyes soaking up every detail. She didn't know who to look at first, her gaze darting between the two cocks jutting out toward her. Sunnie curled her fingers around each shaft and stroked from root to tip. The twin groans from above delivered a thrill that had her tummy fluttering and her sex clenching.

Rand's cock was slightly larger and darker than Z's. Both were on the large size compared to the men of her past, but not in a way that frightened her. Oh no, the length and width had her mouth watering and her pussy weeping. She wasn't the only one leaking. Pearly droplets of precum beaded on both their crowns and Sunnie couldn't resist the temptation. With a swipe of her thumbs she smeared her flesh with the evidence of their arousal and leaned over to lick their essence from her skin.

"Fuck."

The growled curse made her glance up. Rand's hands were fisted at his sides while Z had his curled in his shirt, holding it taut across his abdomen. Bulging muscles stood out on both their arms and necks, and she realized how close to the edge they were. Suddenly aware of their strained control she remembered neither of them had gotten relief in their earlier encounter. With a need that stole her breath, Sunnie set out to remedy the oversight.

Sunnie leaned forward and licked the length of Rand's cock from tip to base and back before sucking the crown between her lips and swiping her tongue over the top. She gripped the shaft to hold him in place and drew in as much of his flesh as she could. All the time her mouth lavished Rand, her other hand worked Z's erection. His hand curled around hers, tightening her fingers and guiding them up and down in ever-increasing strokes.

For long moments Sunnie lost herself in pleasing them. Rand's hips bucked, driving his cock deeper with each lunge between her lips. More precum oozed onto her tongue, and she lapped up every drop. Z had stepped closer, their bodies forming a triangle, making it easier for her to administer to both of them. Letting Rand's slicked-up shaft pop from her mouth, she turned her head and sucked Z's cock into her mouth while dragging her hand up Rand's saliva-covered length.

The musky smell of hot male arousal filled her nose and she continued to alternate between their cocks. Her own juices flowed from her clenching pussy to fill the air with a perfume that held an aphrodisiac quality. As their scents mingled and grew stronger so did her arousal. With each slide of her tongue or hand Sunnie found herself closing in on another orgasm. One she wouldn't have thought possible so quickly after her others. Need turned her movements jerky—desperate—and she soon felt the cock in her mouth pulse against her lips.

With a growl, Z wrapped his fingers in her wet hair and began humping her face. She relaxed her throat and took him as deep as she could, laving his shaft with her tongue on each surge in and out. His grip tightened, the sting sharp as he drove to the back of her mouth and erupted down her throat. Sunnie swallowed, her muscles convulsing in an attempt to drink all he offered. He pulled free, the last of his seed dripping onto her tongue and lips.

Rand gripped her chin and turned her head, his cock pressing against her lips eagerly seeking his own release. Out of breath, Sunnie gasped and received a mouthful of hot flesh and air. He shoved deep, and she had to breathe through her nose or choke. She thought he murmured sorry, but her heart pounded so loud in her ears she couldn't be sure. Rougher than Z, Rand gripped handfuls of hair and used them like reins to drag her mouth over his length. In and out, he sawed between her stretched lips until he shuddered and hot cum spurted from his crown to coat the back of her throat.

"Sunshine."

Her name burst from him on a harsh breath. His hold loosened, and Sunnie dropped back on her heels. The only thing stopping her from falling over was Rand's hand on her shoulder. Her body hummed with unreleased tension. She whimpered, a pleading sound of distress. Slipping her hand between her legs, Sunnie circled her clit with a fingertip, but she didn't get the relief she sought before Z lifted her from the floor.

"No you don't. I want this one."

Z carried her out into the hall and to her room, where he tossed her onto the bed. In seconds, he spread her legs wide and lowered his head to her pussy. The first swipe of his tongue drove her hips up, burying his face deeper into her sex. Z lapped and sucked at her folds, pushing the tip of his tongue as far as he could inside her before torturing her clit with gentle flicks that had her thrashing on the bed. Her leg muscles burned as they were pushed up and back, her knees almost touching the bed next to her ears.

It was the second tongue licking at her pussy that sent her rocking to the edge of bliss. She didn't know how they both managed to get their heads between her legs and didn't care as long as they never stopped. Fingers stroked and probed alongside tongues and lips. From front to back they ate at her until one sensation blurred into another and she could no longer tell what they were doing—only that she'd burst from her skin if she didn't come soon.

Moist heat coated her anus, causing her muscles to clench and bring her back to sanity. Before she could protest, someone sucked on her clit and two fingers thrust deep in her pussy.

Restricted by her position, Sunnie could do nothing but feel. The soft, hot object breaching her ass could only be a tongue and when it pressed deeper she shuddered, nerve endings never before stimulated fired in a rainstorm of soaking intensity. Every part of her concentrated on that one area, and when the pressure retreated she cried out in agonized disappointment.

A chuckle drifted on the air and then the pressure was back. Harder. Thicker. Pressing and pressing until her anus gave way, allowing deeper entry. Stretched and burning, her ass stung with a pleasurable pain she'd never experienced. She wanted it to stop. Not stop. The confusing impulses had her hips rocking into the multiple caresses. Her clit throbbed as wet suction drew it from under its protective hood. Fingers stroked high on the wall of her channel, brushed over that smooth spot of nerves designed to send her into orbit.

Her orgasm broke. Spasms racked her body; her muscles clenched and unclenched in rolling waves that pulled the fingers plying her holes deeper. A scream tore through her throat but barely a sound left her lips as the oxygen was vacuumed from her lungs. The pressure on her clit eased, the fingers in her pussy unmoving as the finger in her ass plunged in and out. Sunnie was completely blindsided by the second, smaller climax that rocketed to life with that rough touch.

"Damn, you're gorgeous. And your ass is so fucking tight. I can't wait to ride it."

Rand's words floated around her mind as she tried to breathe. Gasping with the final pulses of release, her position finally began to hurt. Struggling to speak, Sunnie fought against panic as her vision blurred. Fingers brushed against swollen tissue as they withdrew from her throbbing body. She moaned when her legs were lowered to the bed. Soothing hands rubbed her from ankle to hip as blood flow returned. Sunnie lay there, slowly coming back to normal while the guys continued to run their hands all over her in comforting strokes.

"God, I could watch you come like that for hours," Z said.

"You keep making me come like that and I'll be dead in hours." Sunnie licked her dry lips. "A body can only take so much pleasure."

Rand climbed up on the bed to lie beside her, his head propped on his hand. "You shouldn't lay down a challenge like that, Sunshine. I'd love nothing more than to prove you wrong."

Her eyelids lifted slowly and her lips curled into a smile. "You know, it might just be worth it, but not yet." Her eyes drifted closed again.

"Hey, no time for sleep. We should have been on the road already." Z pinched her nipple.

"Ouch!" Sunnie opened her eyes to give him a dirty look as she slapped his hand away. "And whose fault is that?"

"Yours," they said together.

"What? How's it my fault?" Her gaze darted from one to the other.

"Besides the fact you're too much temptation for one man, never mind two? Getting yourself off without permission would be the big no-no of the day," Rand said.

Sunnie gaped at Rand. Without permission? *What the hell?*

Rand trailed a fingertip along her bottom lip. "It's simple, Sunshine. All you have to do is ask."

Z TOOK the exit for the Central Coast Highway off the F3 Freeway. His brother's house was in Pearl Beach, a tiny beach-side suburb located on a secluded section of the coastline north of the Hawkesbury River. They'd been on the road almost two hours, but if traffic remained light they'd be pulling up to the beach house in about thirty minutes. Just in time for lunch.

Good thing too; his stomach had started rumbling an hour ago. He reached for his water bottle and attempted to pacify his hunger.

It wasn't the only appetite he had, but for now it would be the only one satisfied. Z figured it would be wise to take a step back from the physical connection for a few hours. While there was no doubt they clicked just as well at sex as they did in every other area of their friendship, they needed to learn to combine the two. That's what he hoped their weekend getaway would achieve. He sneaked another glance at Sunnie in the rearview mirror.

Sunnie hadn't argued back at the house, but Z had a feeling there would be hell to pay if Rand bossed her around too much. He was actually looking forward to watching the sparks fly between them, but not at the expense of their relationship. If Rand couldn't learn to dial it back when necessary they'd be banging heads because, as much as Sunnie had seemed to enjoy the bondage, Z didn't believe for one second that she'd be into the whole submissive mindset. She was far too independent for that.

The car interior was cool but the climate-control display showed the outside temperature had already soared to unbearable heights. Once lunch was out of the way he'd suggest a swim. With any luck the beach would be empty. Unlike the public beaches in the area, the one at his brother's back door wasn't accessible to anyone but the row of houses on Gabe's street. And a number of the surrounding properties were home to elderly couples so in all likelihood they'd be the only people around.

"Hey, Rand, wanna check when the storm front is due to come through here?" Z asked.

"It's supposed to hit Sydney around four this afternoon so I would think an hour or so after that, but I'll double-check."

"Did you pack my swimmers?"

Zeke glanced up into the mirror to find Sunnie still staring out the side window, but at least she'd spoken.

"Yep. The blue striped ones."

Her head snapped around, her gaze colliding with his through the glass. "They're too small and you know it."

He smiled as he returned his gaze to the road. They'd been a gift from Sunnie's mother last Christmas. An incentive for her daughter to lose weight, she'd said. From his perspective Sunnie was the perfect size. Tall and stacked, with a chest measurement most women envied and all men wanted to get their hands on, him included. Phoebe Michaels was barely five feet and no bigger than a stick insect, and thought anyone beyond those proportions was obese. Z ground his teeth at the thought of the mind games that woman had played with Sunnie all her life.

Snapping out of his thoughts, he answered Sunnie. "I know you don't think they cover enough of you, but they're more than adequate. To be honest, you look sexy as hell wearing them. I just couldn't resist the thought of you lying on Gabe's secluded beach in those two strips of cloth."

"Whatever."

Z heard Sunnie's sigh and could imagine her rolling her eyes. He laughed but didn't dare look in the mirror again for fear those baby blues would be shooting daggers at him.

"If the beach is deserted you can go without them, Sunshine." Rand turned to look at Sunnie. "Of course, you may not make it out of the house at all."

Sunnie sucked in a breath, and another quick glance in the mirror showed Z she was about to launch both barrels at Rand. As much as he'd been looking forward to the fireworks between his two friends, Z preferred the explosion not take place in the car.

"Oh, no. We're getting out of the house. There's no point driving all this way and not enjoying the beach." Trying to keep his attention on the road as well as the two other occupants of the car, Z chanced a couple of quick looks to be sure the battle wasn't about to begin. Finally he glared in Rand's direction to make it clear he wasn't happy with him, but the bastard only grinned. That's when Z figured out Rand was pushing Sunnie's buttons on purpose. For what reason he couldn't guess but the second they had two minutes together he'd find out.

As Z approached a sharp bend in the road he turned his full concentration back to driving. The curve revealed Broken Bay to their left; the beautiful blue stretch of water eased his breath. He loved the ocean. Everything about it called to him— the sand, the surf, the sun, all important parts of summer life for him since he was a kid. That was why he and Rand got on so well. They often joked about being twins separated at birth. Not surprising that they'd found themselves equally hooked on Sunnie. She wasn't the only one they'd discovered a mutual attraction for over the years, but she'd been the only one they'd kept their hands off.

He drove down the quiet residential street that joined his brother's road. It always made him smile, driving this last stretch of pavement, because he knew in five minutes he'd be relaxing on his brother's back deck looking out over the water and enjoying a cold beer. With a sigh, he swung the car around the last bend and caught a glimpse of crystal blue sea through the trees on the left, a small snippet that was quickly swallowed up by the surrounding trees and houses. When he reached his brother's place he drove into the carport and killed the engine.

"We're here," he said.

"About time. For a man with a V8 supercharged under the hood you sure drive slow." Rand unbuckled his seat belt and opened the door. "The key in the usual spot?"

"Yeah, I'll grab the bag and cooler while you get it." Z slid the keys from the ignition and flung the door open while popping the catch on his belt.

Z hit the button to open the trunk as he climbed out. He pocketed his keys and opened Sunnie's door on his way to the back of the car.

"I'll carry something to the house," Sunnie said as she stepped next to him.

"There's only the cooler and one bag of clothes. I can grab both." Z bent down and grabbed the sports bag. Throwing the straps over his shoulder he hoisted it high and reached for the cooler. "If you want to help, shut the trunk and lock the car. Keys are in my front pocket."

He cocked his right hip toward Sunnie and tried not to drop the bag or cooler. Her hand slid into his pocket and Z froze. Heat from her fingers scorched his skin through the quick-dry material of his board shorts. It only took Sunnie a moment to notice what she was doing and even less time to work the situation to her advantage. Before she removed his keychain he was breathing heavy and threatening to burst out of his pants.

"Not fair, Sunshine," he groaned.

Sunnie smiled. "Life never is." She reached for the trunk lid and slammed it down. With a flick of her wrist she aimed the alarm fob at the car and the telltale double beep told him she'd locked it tight. Picking up her beach tote, she strode off in the direction of the front door.

Z's jaw clenched, his teeth grinding together as he fought to pull himself back under control. The woman had him on the verge of tossing his armload and tackling her to the ground so he could do the one thing they hadn't gotten to yet. Bury his cock in her pussy. He didn't have time to dwell on his problem though. A bigger one presented itself, with a rustle of leaves, a roared obscenity, and a loud crash. Rand fell out of the tree beside the front steps.

"Fuck!" Z dropped the cooler and bag and ran toward his friend.

"Rand. Rand, talk to me." Sunnie knelt, a look of concern on her face.

"I'm. Good," Rand puffed out between his teeth.

"What the hell happened?" Z asked.

"Either I've put on weight," Rand gasped. "Or your brother moved the bird feeder higher up."

Z glanced up into the tree. Sure enough, Gabe had moved the feeder and it now sat in the smaller branches. He looked back down at Rand.

"Think you can get up?"

"Yeah. Give me a hand."

He offered his hand and waited for Rand to get a good grip. When his friend gave the nod, Z slowly eased him to his feet. At first he thought Rand might fall but Sunnie quickly wrapped her arm around Rand's waist and let him lean on her shoulder. Not that Z thought she was actually holding up the six foot two inch frame that was their friend. Nope. Rand was milking the fall for all it was worth. Z grinned and went back for their gear.

"In all that drama did you even get the key?" he called over his shoulder.

"Yes, thank God. There's no way I'm risking life and limb again," Rand said as Sunnie helped him up the three front steps.

"Want me to call an ambulance to take your pansy-ass to the emergency room?" Z chuckled at the dirty looks both his friends sent in his direction.

"Z, have some sympathy." Sunnie glared at him with narrowed eyes.

"Sure, sure. Just get the key off him and open the door. This thing is damn heavy."

Sunnie pushed the door open and helped Rand inside to the couch before racing around the house to open windows and doors to let some of the stale, hot air out. She took off upstairs when she had the ground level done. The sea breeze blew in through the deck doors and Z sucked in a deep breath.

"Damn that smells good."

"Yeah, it does." Rand turned to look out the patio doors. "And get a load of that view. Why don't we come up here more often?"

"Don't know. I'm starting to wonder why I don't take my brother's advice and buy a place up here." Z walked over to the kitchen area and set down the cooler just as Sunnie came back downstairs. "Sunnie, want to help me unpack the food and get some lunch together while the bird with the clipped wing rests his sorry ass?"

She frowned at him but didn't reprimand him for calling Rand more names. "What did you pack in the way of food?"

"Let's see." Z lifted the lid and started removing food. "Steak, salad, ham."

"I threw in a frozen pizza too," Rand said.

"You think it's still frozen?" Sunnie's right eyebrow arched.

"No, I guess not," Rand murmured.

"Did you bring any bread to make sandwiches with?" Sunnie asked.

"Shit. I knew we had to stop for something." Z pulled out the pizza box and ripped open the end. What came out didn't look too appetizing. As it thawed all the toppings had slipped to one side because Rand had stupidly packed the box on its end, not flat. "Crap."

"Here. Give me that." Sunnie snatched the defrosted pizza from his hands. "You go down to the shop and get either fresh bread rolls or a loaf of bread. By the time you get back I'll have everything ready to eat."

"Are you sure?" He glanced at Rand. "I'm happy to fix it all when I get back."

"I'm sure." She started to cut open the plastic wrap on the pizza. "Take Rand with you. He looks fully recovered to me."

"I think we've been dismissed, Z." Rand pushed from the couch. "Do we want anything other than bread?"

Sunnie rummaged through the rest of the cooler contents. "Nope, looks as though you've got everything else covered."

"Okay, we'll be back in ten." Z kissed Sunnie on the lips. "So you don't forget me while I'm gone."

Rand walked over and mimicked Z's move. "Or me."

They left the house with Sunnie staring openmouthed after them.

6

SUNNIE HADN'T MEANT to run them out of the house earlier, but she'd needed space and she wasn't getting any with them around. She was certain they didn't intend for her to feel smothered, but that's exactly how she felt. Like someone had wrapped ribbon around her chest impossibly tight, restricting her air intake. They were longer than ten minutes at the shop and she hadn't a clue what was said, but since their return the day had taken on an easier tone. The nerve-racking tension of earlier had gone, much to her relief.

They'd enjoyed a leisurely lunch on the deck before changing into their swimmers and heading down to the beach. Rand and Z were swimming about fifty feet from shore while Sunnie sat in the cool, wet sand at the water's edge letting the gentle waves roll over her feet. She was in the dreaded swimsuit—the one that barely covered her. Like the pinup girls of the last century, Sunnie had curves and an impressive bustline. Sunnie smiled. She might not be comfortable in the bikini but even she had to admit she looked hot in it. Her mother couldn't undermine Sunnie's confidence in her body image no matter how many tiny bathing suits she bought her.

Unfortunately her mother had the ability to make her doubt every other aspect of herself. From her career choice to her taste in ice cream flavors, Phoebe Michaels could destroy Sunnie with a few words. And why the hell was she thinking about her mother now? She had far more enjoyable things to contemplate. Starting with the two sexy men currently swimming back to shore. Sunnie dug her fingers and toes into the soggy sand and pushed to her feet.

"Last one back to the house has to do the dishes," she yelled before she took off up the beach.

Sunnie made it up the stairs and to the patio doors before they caught her. Unprepared for the tackle that took her down, she lost her breath and the rest was squished out of her when two solid, dripping wet bodies sprawled on top of her. Pinned beneath them she gasped for air until they scrambled off and dragged her from the floor.

"You okay?"

"Where does it hurt?"

Two sets of hands roamed her body searching for injury. They squeezed and stroked, checking her limbs with exaggerated care. But the simple touches soon changed; the long sweeps and gentle probes turned erotic, sending chills and goose bumps in every direction, and Sunnie became breathless for a completely different reason.

"Damn, Sunshine, tell me you're not hurt," Z growled in her ear. He nuzzled the sensitive spot on her neck just below her jawline, and a shiver raced down her spine.

"Tell us." Rand followed his demand with the scrape of his teeth over her collarbone.

"I-I'm fine." Words left her lips on shaky breath.

"Bathroom." Z lifted her off her feet. "We need to wash off the sand and salt."

She clung to his neck and stared at Rand as he followed them deeper into the house and up the stairs. When Z placed her feet on the bath mat her knees shook, threatening to give way, but Rand gripped her elbow to steady her while Z started up the water.

"Shit. I forgot Gabe said the hot water wasn't working."

"Then we better make this quick," Rand said.

Z sucked a breath through his teeth when he stepped under the spray. Sunnie shuddered at the thought of a cold shower. She liked hers on the hot side, even in the middle of summer, but there was no escaping this necessary wash down. She turned to see Rand, grim faced, stripping off and getting ready to follow Z.

"After you," Rand said.

"Oh God." Sunnie leaped forward. "Aargh..."

Any breath she may have caught in the last few minutes instantly evaporated. The water wasn't just cold; it was damn near freezing. Goose bumps broke out all over her body, her nipples turned to rock-hard nubs beneath her swimmers, and shivers rattled her bones from head to toe.

"Move over. Let's get this done." Rand squeezed in behind her, his body warm against her back.

"G-good th-thing your b-brother has a b-big sh-sh-shower." Sunnie's words were punctuated by the clacking of her chattering teeth.

"Fuck. It's worse than Bondi in winter." Rand reached passed Sunnie and grabbed the soap. He quickly lathered his hands and offered her the bar. "Here, pass the soap around."

Sunnie's fingers were shaking so much she couldn't hold on to the slippery bar and the small square shot off into the wall before falling to the floor. "S-sorry."

"Don't worry. We'll take care of you first," Z said.

Dropping to his knees, Z retrieved the soap and began washing her legs at the same time Rand cupped her shoulders. Together they rinsed away the sand and salt from her body, removing her swimsuit as they went. Sunnie was so cold she couldn't protest or enjoy their efforts. Not even when Z stroked her breasts and between her legs, or when Rand wove his fingers through her hair. All she could do was tremble and listen to her teeth chattering. As soon as they were satisfied she was clean Rand gripped her waist and lifted her out onto the mat.

"Grab a towel and dry off," Z said as he stripped out of his shorts and washed.

Her hands shook as she reached for the closest towel, but she managed to hold on and get it wrapped around her torso. Grabbing a second towel, Sunnie rubbed her hair and then twirled it turban style on her head. The shaking had subsided to small tremors, but her fingers and toes remained numb. She was still trying to dry off when Z and Rand joined her on the mat. They wasted no time in wiping their own wet bodies and were soon rubbing off the last of the moisture clinging to hers.

"Come on, let's get you warm." Rand ushered her out of the chilly room and across the hall into the main bedroom.

The bag with their clothes sat by the wall. Ignoring it, Rand herded her toward the big bed that took up more than half the floor space. Z whipped the covers back and turned to tug the towels from her head and body. Tossing the soggy bundle on the hardwood floor, he knelt on the mattress and pulled her after him.

"Why are we getting into bed?"

"Quickest way to get warm is body heat," Rand said, as he patted her ass and crawled after her.

"Oh."

Sunnie followed Z across the bed until they were stretched out in the middle of the huge expanse of pale green sheet. Rand slid up behind her, his body curving along hers. Warm summer air filled the room and with Z plastered to her front and Rand at her back, she soon warmed up. But warm quickly became hot. Surrounded neck to ankle by their nakedness had interesting things popping up—in and *out* of her mind. She'd never been in a situation like this and as much as her head was screaming no, her body yelled yes twice as loud.

For long minutes they lay in silence, each lost in their own thoughts until Sunnie couldn't help but move her hand along Z's skin. She had one arm tucked up under her head, while the other was draped over Z's side. Her fingers began to trace the line of his spine. Sunnie flattened her hand, her skin touching his from wrist to fingertips, and pressed into the hard muscles of his upper back. Z murmured something into her hair but she couldn't make out the words and didn't care because Rand had begun an exploration of his own.

Rand's fingers skimmed over the curve of her hip and down her thigh while his lips spread tiny kisses across her shoulder. She arched into Rand's touch and her breasts pressed against Z's chest, her nipples tightening at the hot, hard contact. Z worked his hand between them, his fingers splayed over her ribs, his thumb barely brushing the underside of one breast and Sunnie whimpered with the need for more.

"Okay?" Z murmured in her hair as he finally took the full weight of her breast in his palm.

Her back bowed and a moan slipped from her throat as streamers of warmth radiated out from his caress. He pinched her nipple, tugged on the knot of nerves, making her gasp. Fire streaked through her and delivered a searing heat to her core. Need flared, bright and urgent, and slashed at her insides. She squirmed between them, her body seeking their touch and the satisfaction she knew they'd bring her.

"Easy, Sunshine." Rand nipped at her ear, his teeth and lips toying with the fleshy lobe. "There's no rush."

No rush? With every fiber of her being she disagreed. The fervent yearning blazing a trail along her skin argued her point. Sunnie wiggled her ass, her cheeks cradling Rand's length while her pussy clenched in want. She'd never craved sex like this. Never longed to be filled with such wicked desire that it stole her breath—her sanity.

"Now." She thrust her hips back harder. "I need."

"Shh..." Z soothed her with soft kisses on her temple. "Relax. We've got all night."

Jesus, they were going to kill her with their restraint. Her body tightened with every brush of skin on skin, the slightest touch enflaming her arousal until Sunnie knew she'd get off with the barest stroke on her clit. Tremors rocked her as she undulated between them, her mind and body seeking the orgasm it desperately craved. She threw her leg over Z's and ground her pussy on his thigh.

"No you don't." Rand slid his arms around her waist and rolled, pulling her away from Z. "No getting off without asking, Sunnie."

"What? No!" She squirmed on top of him, tried to break free of his grip.

"Rand." Z's face appeared above her. His eyes flashed with concern. "Let's all take a breath." He brushed the hair from her forehead.

"Dammit. Let me go." Sunnie dug an elbow into Rand's stomach and was pleased to hear the rush of air that escaped his chest.

His hold loosened and she scrambled off him into Z's arms. She clung like her life depended on it. The wild lust still sang in her veins, pounding in her ears and warring with the sudden change in mood. This was all so confusing, so wrong. Rand had always been the gentler of her two friends, but it was Z who soothed her. How could they be such complete opposites in bed? And why did the demands Rand expected turn her on— make her want to obey? Sunnie shivered in Z's embrace, her arousal going from a roar to a hum as he rocked her.

RAND STARED into his best friend's eyes and knew he'd screwed up. He'd scared Sunnie. She clung to Z like a leech and Rand wanted to kick his own ass, never mind receiving the clear message that Z planned to do just that in the near future. He scrubbed a hand down his face and blew out a breath of air. First thing he had to do was apologize to Sunnie. Pushing off the mattress, he sat up and placed a hand on the back of her head. The fact she didn't flinch was a good sign.

"I'm sorry." Rand knew the words weren't enough. He had to show her he wasn't a caveman, that even though he'd demand things from her, he'd never hurt her and would stop when she asked.

He stroked her hair, the blonde strands flowing over his fingers as he tried to find the right way to explain not only his behavior but his desires as well. He'd never questioned his sexual urges, but now, looking at Sunnie trembling in Z's arms, he had to wonder why. It was probably the fact no woman had ever pulled away from him before. And no one had brought out the need to control like Sunnie. Rand imagined there would be plenty of wrong steps before they completely meshed their new relationship.

Rand leaned forward and slid his arms around Sunnie. With a gentle tug he pulled her from Z's hold and drew her into his lap. He tucked her head beneath his chin and held her close but not too tightly. For long moments they sat in silence. Z continued to give him a dark stare but remained quiet. She'd curled into his chest when he first picked her up, and Rand thanked his lucky stars that she didn't appear afraid of him physically.

"I'm sorry." Rand kissed the top of her head.

"I know." She spoke against his chest, her breath tickling the hair and surrounding his nipple with warmth.

"If anything I do, in or out of bed, scares you all you have to do is say so."

"You didn't scare me."

He thought he'd misheard her words and his gaze shot up to meet Z's. "Then what happened? You were shaking like a leaf and fighting against me."

Sunnie ducked her head, hiding her face from view, making it hard for him or Z to read her expression. Rand shifted his hold, moved her around a little so he could tip her head up to look at her. Her cheeks were flushed red and her eyelids hung low, concealing her eyes.

"If it wasn't fear, what was it, Sunshine?" Rand cupped her jaw, stroked his thumb over her bottom lip.

Her eyelids fluttered up, the long blonde lashes fanning out to frame the blue orbs swirling with heat—lust. Rand's cock jerked to attention and he sucked in a breath at the blatant look of need she couldn't hide. He turned to Z, who was watching Sunnie with quiet intensity.

"Damn. You're not scared. You're horny," Z said. His friend reached over and cupped the opposite side of her face.

"Why'd you fight against me if you didn't want to get away?" Rand didn't understand; she'd shown all the signs of fear, but there wasn't a trace of it now.

"I wasn't trying to get away. I was trying to jump one of

you." The color in her cheeks deepened but she stuck her chin up in challenge.

"You wanted to jump one of us?"

She scrambled out of Rand's lap and bounced across the bed. Throwing her legs over the edge Sunnie sprang to her feet and spun around to face them, her hands firmly planted on her hips.

"What did you expect? You had your hands all over me and the heat coming off your naked bodies was enough to fry my brain never mind boil my blood."

Rand's cock stood at full mast. The sight of Sunnie, in all her naked glory, giving them what for did a number on his libido. He glanced down and saw the bead of precum oozing from his slit. Oh yeah, she had him.

"It was fucking cruel to snatch that away from me," Sunnie said.

He hadn't heard half of what she said; all he knew was that he wanted her back on the bed and pressed beneath him, his cock buried inside her. Rand turned to Z. His friend was fighting a similar battle to hold back. Why did they bother to fight their desire at all? She wanted them. They wanted her. Simple. Turning back to Sunnie, he hopped off the bed and started toward her.

"Why are you looking at me like that?" She backed up a step, her hands lifting from her hips.

Rand didn't answer. He continued to stalk her like the prey his ravenous hunger thought she was.

"Rand?" Sunnie took another step back, her fingers twisting together in front of her.

He didn't stop. While she was focused on him, Z circled around until the only place for her to go was into the wall behind her or through their barricade of flesh. And she wasn't getting past that in this lifetime.

"Z?"

She'd brought one hand up in the universal signal for them to stop, but Rand saw the way her gaze dropped to their hard cocks, saw the way she licked her lips before looking them in the eyes again. He got within arm's length of her outstretched hand and, in a blur of motion, slipped his fingers around her wrist to pull her into him. With her chest plastered to his, her erect nipples rivaled his erect cock for hardness as he bucked his hips against her. Z stepped in behind her, pinning her between them. Sunnie gasped, her pupils dilating until Rand could hardly make out the blue.

"If you don't want this, Sunshine, tell us now." Rand kept his gaze on hers, watched for any sign she wasn't one hundred percent into this.

When she didn't answer him, he pressed his hard on into her softness. Rand bent his head and tongued her ear, tracing the outer shell before sucking the lobe into his mouth and nipping with his teeth.

"Yes or no, Sunnie." Z spoke from the other side of her head.

Sunnie moaned and Rand guessed Z was giving the other side of her neck some attention while he kissed and licked this side. He dragged the edge of his teeth down the gentle slope of her throat, his tongue bathing the pulse pounding in the hollow at the base.

"We need an answer, Sunshine. Yes or no." Rand spoke against her skin, the area heating beneath his breath.

"Y-yes."

He gripped her waist and, bringing her with him, walked backward until his calves bumped into the mattress. Raising his head, he gazed into her eyes and asked one more time.

"Are you sure?"

A slight inclination of her head was his only warning. Her

face drew closer and in the next breath she was sharing his air. She slanted her mouth over his, her tongue snaking out to probe the seam of his lips until he opened and allowed her in. Rand loved the way she kissed. With demand and need, she gave herself over to him. He'd never experienced any kiss like it. Take and surrender in one action. The lush slide of her flesh on his sent heat rushing through his veins until every part of his body caught fire.

Rand tore his mouth from hers and gasped for breath. His chest heaved and his balls ached with the need to unload. He spun Sunnie around and tossed her onto the bed. She didn't get a chance to move before he was on top of her, his body pressing hers into the mattress, his cock cradled by her pussy. The heat of her flesh scorched him and when he rocked against her his shaft slid with ease along her slick folds.

"God, I can't wait to fuck you." Rand flexed his hips and his cock probed deeper, the head searching out the silken hole waiting for him.

Sunnie rolled her hips beneath him and he sucked in a breath when his body breached hers. Wet, hot, tight. She surrounded him and Rand nearly lost it there and then. He pulled back, drove forward, and sank a little deeper inside her. It blew his mind how good it felt to be skin on skin with her. The thought brought him up short.

"Shit!"

"What?" Sunnie gasped as he abruptly pulled from her body.

"Condom," Z said right before a foil packet dropped on the sheet beside Sunnie's head.

Rand pushed to his knees when she dropped her legs from around him. With unsteady hands, he tore the wrapper open and removed the condom.

"Here, let me." Sunnie plucked the rubber from his nerveless fingers.

He sucked air through his teeth as she rolled the condom down his length. Shudders racked his spine and he wasted no time getting back inside her once the protection was in place. Rand placed a hand between her breasts and shoved her back on the bed. Slipping his arms beneath her knees, he raised her legs and aimed for home. One hard, fast thrust and he was buried balls deep.

Sunnie gasped at his sudden invasion and he held still, his muscles straining, to give her a moment to adjust. But the heat of her tore at the leash he had on his control and, within seconds, he knew he couldn't hold off any longer. He buried his face in the soft skin of her throat and withdrew.

"Sorry," he murmured against her skin. "Can't. Hold. Back."

Rand took her then. Hard and fast he drove in and out of her tightness. She moaned and thrashed under him, her inner muscles squeezing him tighter with every pass through her swollen flesh. He let go of her legs and she wrapped them around him, her heels digging into his ass as she spurred him on. In an embarrassing amount of time he reached the point of no return. But going over the edge before her was out of the question. Tunneling a hand between them, Rand searched out the knot of nerves that would guarantee her climax.

Sunnie bucked beneath him when he hit pay dirt. He circled the hard bundle with his fingertip and as the first tremor of her release rippled down his length he quickened his pace, added pressure, and sent her flying. Her pussy clamped onto his cock like a vise, the silken walls sucking at him and dragging him with her. With a roar of satisfaction he came. Surge after surge of cum filled the condom. When the final spurt left his body he collapsed to the side. Struggling to keep his full weight off her, he used the last of his energy to roll over, taking her with him.

"Jesus Christ, that was the hottest fucking thing I've ever seen."

Z's voice broke through the fog of his orgasm. Rand smiled. Watching may have been hot, but doing was fucking scorching.

"My turn," his friend growled.

Z COULD BARELY CONTROL HIMSELF. He'd sheathed his cock while watching Rand fuck Sunnie and the routine act pushed him so close to blowing his load he'd had to squeeze the base of his shaft to stop himself from coming before he got inside her. He gripped her waist and lifted her from Rand's chest. Placing her face-down on the mattress beside his friend, Z dragged his hands over the dip of her waist to her hips, dug his fingers into her flesh, and pulled back until she was on her knees, ass up. The sight of her well-fucked pussy, all wet and glistening, had more blood rushing into his cock.

With his hands on her thighs, he urged Sunnie's legs farther apart. He wedged his knees between hers and, with one hand wrapped around his cock to hold it steady, he lined up the head and pressed inside her. Hot and wet, her walls sucked at his shaft until he was buried to the hilt. Z gripped her hips, his fingers curling into the supple curves as he held on to control by a thread. Nostrils flaring, he pulled in a deep breath and was instantly sent careening into madness. The air, ripe with sex, filled his chest and threw his lust into overdrive.

He withdrew from her clinging channel and slammed back in. The slide of slick tissue over his aching shaft drove him further into insanity and closer to release. Hard and fast, he powered his body into hers, each buck of his hips impaling and withdrawing his cock quicker and quicker until his balls burned with need. Nothing mattered more than bringing them both to the peak. Z leaned over, his chest connecting with her damp back, and letting go of one hip he moved his hand under them to find her clit.

The hard knot of nerves stood tall between the wet folds of her slit. He circled, flicked, circled again. Z teased her—tortured them both—with every stroke. Her pussy quivered around his cock as her orgasm approached. Capturing the slippery pearl between his fingers, he pinched lightly and sent her over the edge. Heat soaked through the rubber to scald his length as her sex flooded with her release. She thrashed beneath him, her hips jerking against his, pressing the soft cheeks of her ass into him.

Z growled with each thrust, pushing wave after wave of hot cream out of her convulsing pussy to coat his balls. The slap-slap of flesh on flesh quickened as he reared up and drove into her harder. Faster. *Harder.* His sac tightened in response to the walls of her sex clamping his cock within their heated depths, and her orgasm held them both in its powerful grip. He clenched his jaw, ground his teeth in an attempt to hold off the inevitable. But it was no use. Prickly heat burst in his groin, shot up his spine and down his legs as his body reached breaking point.

He came, hard and fast, just like he'd fucked her. His pelvis bucked and jerked as he spilled his seed, his hips snug against hers. Shuddering with his release, Z collapsed forward with a grunt and pressed Sunnie into the mattress below. Breathing hard, he held as much of his weight as he could on his elbows, but his muscles shook with spent energy and he knew he had to roll off her before they gave way.

Pushing up on shaky limbs, Z pulled from Sunnie's still pulsing body and fell to the side. His chest heaved and his lungs stung as he gasped for air. He turned to look at Sunnie.

Rand lay on her other side, his head propped on one hand while the other hand glided up and down her spine in sweeping caresses. She faced Z, eyes closed, with lashes spiked with moisture. He reached over and ran his fingertip through the wetness.

"Sunshine?" Z traced his finger over the bridge of her nose to her other eye.

"Mmm..." Her eyelids fluttered open to reveal pools of swimming blue.

"You're crying?" he asked.

"What?" Rand leaned over to see her better.

She smiled the most serene smile Z had ever seen. "Don't panic. I'm not crying."

"But?" Z swiped at the liquid beneath her eye.

"Did we hurt you?" Rand asked as he gripped her chin and tipped her face up.

"No." She licked her lips. "Neither of you hurt me."

"Then why are you crying?" Z asked.

"It's a physical reaction to the mind-blowing orgasms you both gave me." She cupped his jaw in her hand. "I can't explain it. It's never happened to me before, but I'm not in pain or sad. Far from it."

Z searched her eyes and breathed a sigh of relief when he realized she was telling the truth. The thought of hurting her tore into his heart. He'd never forgive himself if he caused her pain—physical or emotional. "You'd tell us if we did hurt you, right?"

Sunnie ran her thumb along his bottom lip, causing a tremor to roll down his spine. "You'll be the first to know."

"So are they happy tears?" Rand asked.

Her gaze left Z and moved to Rand. "Mmm, yeah, that's probably the best way to describe them."

"You don't sound convinced." Z said.

She brought her gaze back to his. "That's because I've never felt like this before. Happy doesn't even begin to cover it."

Z's chest puffed up at her comment.

Sunnie yawned. "Jeez, you guys wore me out. I'm just gonna lie here a while."

He leaned forward and brushed his lips on hers before pulling back. "Take a nap. I'll go down and get dinner started."

Her hand snapped out and grabbed his wrist. "No. Don't go. Stay with me."

"It's getting late. We should start getting dinner organized," Rand said.

"Not hungry." Sunnie yawned.

Z laughed. "You will be when you wake up."

"Don't care. Stay." Another yawn. "Both of you."

He combed the hair from her face with his fingers. "Okay, for a little while."

"No. Not a little while." She moved into Z's touch, wiggled backward until she pressed her body into Rand's and murmured, "Forever."

7

Z PICKED up the first steak and placed it on the hot grill. He couldn't get Sunnie's plea out of his head. *Forever.* That one word had choked him up good. He'd love nothing more than spending forever with her and Rand, but he wasn't sure she even knew she'd let the request slip. She'd come downstairs about ten minutes ago, dressed in the sweatpants and top he'd packed for her. It wasn't cold, so he couldn't help thinking she felt the need to cover up—hide.

During their lovemaking—and it was making love, no matter how raw and primal the encounter had been—emotions had played a major part in every move, and the whole thing had been overwhelming. The blind rush of desperate need to have a woman, the need to take all she was, had never been a part of sex before. Not for him. Not even with the women he thought he'd loved. Nothing compared to the depth of feeling Z had for Sunnie.

She remained quiet, sitting in a deck chair with her legs tucked up underneath her, staring out at the water. The predicted storm hadn't arrived yet, but Z noticed dark clouds moving in from the south as he turned the steaks. In another few minutes the meat would be ready to come off the barbecue. Rand walked over and offered him a beer. They sipped and watched as the day dulled with the setting sun and the coming storm.

"Should we be worried?" Rand murmured, tilting his head in Sunnie's direction.

Z glanced over at her. "I'm not sure."

"She hasn't said a word since she declined a drink."

"I know." Z brought his gaze back to his friend. "But I can't think of anything to say that won't send her screaming from the house."

Rand looked at him. "What do you want to say?"

He sighed. "That I love her."

"Jesus, thank God." Rand dropped his head and stared at the timber decking. "I thought it was just me."

"No." Z smiled ruefully. "There's definitely two of us feeling it. But I don't know about Sunnie."

Raising his head, Rand looked Z in the eye. "Do you honestly think she would have agreed to any of this if she didn't love us?"

Z shook his head. "No. But she's always loved us, Rand. The question is will she risk being *in love* with us."

Rand blew a breath out through his lips. "Damn. This isn't going to be easy, is it?"

"The best things are worth fighting for."

"We'll never win if she fights against us."

"Sure we will." Z smiled as he moved the meat from the grill onto a plate. "It's two against one."

Rand's bark of laughter had Sunnie looking in their direction. Z held the plate of meat as he switched off the burners then headed inside.

"Dinner's ready," he said on his way through the door.

Z placed the steaks on the table as he passed on his way to the kitchen. He pulled the salad from the fridge and grabbed the bottle of red wine he'd left breathing on the counter. Returning to the dining area he found Rand helping Sunnie into a chair. She picked the smallest piece of meat and put it on her plate before drowning it in ketchup.

"Jeez, Sunnie, do you have to ruin a good piece of steak like that?" Rand asked as he sat.

She shrugged but didn't utter a word. Instead she sliced into the meat and popped a bite into her mouth. Z watched with amusement as she proceeded to cut her steak into bite-size portions. Smiling, he focused his attention on his own meal and tried to come up with a neutral topic of conversation. But nothing broke through the swirl of thoughts currently spinning in his mind. The main dilemma was convincing Sunnie that what they offered could fit the happy-ever-after mold, even if it was a misshapen one.

He continued to mull over ideas as he ate. Bite after bite went in his mouth and down his throat, but he tasted none of it. And the wine was nothing more than a way to wash down the food. Rand tried to get Sunnie talking, but her answers remained minimal. Z wondered if she regretted going to bed with them. When she placed her knife and fork together on her plate that was over half full, he really began to worry.

"Are you okay, Sunshine? You've hardly eaten a thing," Z said.

"Not really hungry." She pushed her chair back, picking up her dish and glass as she stood. "I'll start washing up."

Z watched her walk away, the sway of her hips drawing his gaze. When she reached the kitchen he turned to Rand. "I don't know how to snap her out of the daze she seems to have fallen in. Do you think she regrets what happened?"

"I'm leaning more toward kicking herself for enjoying it so much." Rand shrugged. "She's a little embarrassed by it, I think. She hasn't looked either of us in the eye."

"Hmm, I guess we could give her some space." Z glanced over at Sunnie. "But she's not going to be happy when we all pile in the same bed tonight."

"Maybe we can pull her out of her funk before then."

"Any idea how?"

"How 'bout we find something funny to watch from Gabe's collection? Lighten the mood a bit."

"Good idea. You help her with the dishes, and I'll set up a movie."

"Oh no, your movie choices are shit. You do the dishes. *I'll* get the movie ready." Rand stood. "Do you think Gabe has any microwave popcorn in the cupboard?"

"Don't know. I'll check. He usually has the place pretty well stocked."

Z stacked the plates and took them to the kitchen. He scraped and rinsed before handing them to Sunnie to load in the machine.

"Rand's picking a movie for us to watch." He tried to engage her, but she wasn't having any of it.

"Okay."

He sighed. It was going to be one long-ass night if they couldn't snap her out of this weird mood. Heading back to the table for the wineglasses, he prayed they'd find a way but he wasn't averse to using their sexual chemistry and trying to seduce her out it. The thought sent a tingle down his spine and tightened his balls. Regardless of this setback, Z was still optimistic they could make this three-way relationship work. They just needed time to adjust to the newness of their physical connection.

•   •   •

SUNNIE KNEW she was behaving strangely, but she couldn't help it. They'd given her more than great sex. The physical side of their encounter was the easiest part to understand and get her head around. Both of them were skilled lovers and weren't afraid to use their knowledge, but neither of them had held back their emotions while sending her through the roof with pleasure. That was the bit she couldn't wrap her mind around. While they'd each taken her with a feral need she'd never experienced before, she hadn't felt used. Just the opposite. She'd felt loved—cherished. And now she was awash with conflicting emotions.

The whole shift in their relationship overwhelmed her. No one loved her unconditionally except her fathers, and that was such a tangled web of emotions that even at twenty-seven Sunnie hadn't come to terms with having the three men in her life. Her mother, on the other hand, had taught her that everything, including love, came at a price. One of Phoebe's favorite nuggets of wisdom was *nothing is ever free*. With Phoebe everything came with strings and expectations—conditions.

Why couldn't she be normal? Why couldn't she accept what Rand and Z offered without all the doubt and fear? She'd grown up with three doting fathers, so surely that would lead her to believe two men could love her equally, and that she could love them equally in return. But the relationship between her fathers and Phoebe was anything but loving. The battleground that had been Sunnie's childhood frightened and upset her as though she were still that little girl caught in the tug-of-war her mother enjoyed. Phoebe had thrived on the drama and used Sunnie at every opportunity to get at her fathers.

Sunnie sighed and curled her legs tighter to her chest. She'd sunk down in one of the soft armchairs while Rand and Z sat on the big couch. Neither of them had commented when she hadn't joined them on the couch to watch the movie. Rand had picked a comedy, although none of them had found it all that funny. Then again, Sunnie wasn't really watching—more like staring off into space. Her mind wouldn't stop spinning with thought after thought. Nothing made sense. Not her fear, her excitement, or the bone-deep emotion she knew was love for the two men across the room. She'd always loved them, but this was different—deeper—an all-consuming feeling that threatened to drown her.

"Sunshine?"

Z's raised voice snapped Sunnie out of her daze. She blinked rapidly. The TV screen was blank. When had the movie finished? Rand's hand waved back and forth in front of her face.

"Earth to Sunnie. Earth to Sunnie."

She sucked in a breath at their nearness. They were standing right in front of her chair and she hadn't even seen them move.

"You asleep with your eyes open?" Z asked as he reached down and grabbed her hand. "Come on. Time for bed, I think."

Sunnie froze, her gaze darting between the two of them. "But...but I'm not tired." She punctuated the lie with a yawn.

Rand laughed. "Oh yeah, we see that." He bent forward and placed his hand under her chin, tipped her head up, and held her firmly so she couldn't turn away. "Relax, Sunshine. Nothing happens without your consent. Ever."

He waited for her to nod before he leaned over and brushed his lips across hers, a light peck that had her hormones dancing with glee. Sunnie squashed them as best she could. She wasn't ready to go there again, not by a long shot. Her confusion cast a dark cloud over the three of them and she wished with all her heart that it didn't have to be that way. But there was no controlling the emotions besieging her and, until she could clear her mind, she'd have to ignore any demands her body made.

"Come on." Z pulled her to her feet. "Nothing more than three people sharing the same bed to sleep in."

Sunnie shivered. The last time the three of them had crawled into bed together they'd done many things. Sleep wasn't one of them. But the looks on their faces convinced her they would honor their words. There'd be no sex without her asking for it. And why did that thought send a curl of disappointment through her? She really did need to make up her mind about what she wanted. Or maybe she just needed to tell her head to shut up and listen to her heart and body, because those two were in perfect agreement.

Rand's hand pressed against her back, guiding her as Z pulled her behind him, his grip on her hand gentle but firm. They switched off lights as they made their way upstairs. She'd obviously been zoned out completely because she'd missed them locking up downstairs. With nerves skittering like a plague of mice, Sunnie found it hard to catch her breath. The closer they got to the bedroom the more anxious she became. She knew what she'd see when they entered the room. A king-size bed with sex-rumpled sheets. A shiver ran down her spine.

"Cold?" Rand asked.

"What?" She glanced over her shoulder. "No, not really."

His gaze softened and he slid his hand up along her spine until his palm cupped her nape. "Relax, Sunshine. You're safe with us, no matter what happens."

She knew that. Knew they'd protect her as best they could. But how would they stop her from hurting herself? From hurting *them*? Sunnie might not know how she felt about everything that was happening between them, but she was sure none of them would get out of this unscathed. With a slight nod she turned her gaze away and stared at Z's back as they walked along the short hallway. A few steps away from the door, Sunnie sucked in a breath and held it. Her fingers trembled in Z's, and she hoped he couldn't feel them or hear her pounding heart.

Rand's hand disappeared from her back a second before both his hands curled over her shoulders and he leaned forward. "Sunshine, if you keep holding your breath like that you're gonna pass out. Breathe." He gave her a gentle squeeze before letting go.

The room was dark when they entered, but Z didn't bother with the light switch. Instead, he tugged her across the room to the bed, pulled her around in front of him and guided her onto the mattress.

"Scoot over to the middle." Z followed her, stretching out on his side.

Rand walked to the foot of the bed and grabbed the covers they'd kicked off earlier. With a flick of his wrists he spread the blanket over her and Z. A flash of light lit the room as Rand crawled onto the bed beside her. Sunnie's gaze darted to the wall of windows the bed faced as a clap of thunder shook the house and scared the shit out of her.

Sunnie slapped a hand over her mouth to stifle her scream.

Z laughed. "Looks like the storm finally hit. We're in for an amazing show."

"What?" Sunnie removed her trembling hand and burrowed farther under the covers as if they could offer protection from the fury being unleashed outside.

"Here." Z fluffed up her pillow. "Lean up against the headboard and relax. Watching Mother Nature let loose is one of the best sights in the world."

"You're kidding?" Sunnie wanted to pull the blanket over her head and not come out until the storm had passed. "I'd prefer to close the blinds."

Rand finish propping up his pillow and settled next to her. "Z's right. There's nothing more thrilling than watching a lightning storm."

"I can think of plenty," she mumbled under her breath as she wiggled a little lower on the bed.

"Come here." Z wrapped his arm around her shoulders and tugged her closer. "Honestly, there's nothing to worry about. It's not like you haven't seen a storm before."

"I've never seem one from inside a goldfish bowl."

"A goldfish bowl?" Rand chuckled.

"Hey, that whole wall is windows. You can't tell me it doesn't remind you of a goldfish bowl," she argued, waving her hand at the offending glass.

"Think of it more like a real-life Imax theatre. You loved it when we went to that showing of the arctic animals last month," Z reminded her.

"Yes, but that was from the safety of a well-cushioned chair with an exit door to the right." Sunnie squirmed as another flash of light flooded the room.

"Here's a thought," Rand said. "This is a well-padded mattress and the exit door is still just to your right." He patted the bed between them and pointed to the bedroom door.

Rand was right; she knew that, but she hated lightning storms. She'd had an irrational fear of them her whole life and without fail, whenever one occurred, she would instantly find somewhere that allowed her to remain oblivious to the flashes of electricity. Growing up, her safe haven had been the closet in her room. She would drag her toys in with her and play in the dark for hours. As she'd gotten older—and wiser—she'd managed to convince herself that closing the blinds or curtains on all the windows was enough protection. Sunnie figured if she was ever going to outgrow the terror it would have happened by now.

"Snuggle in closer." Z tightened his hold. "You're shaking. Are you cold?"

Sunnie edged as close as she could without crawling on top of Z, and when Rand's warm body pressed into her other side she felt marginally better. Surrounded with their warmth, she found the courage to admit her fear.

"I'm terrified of lightning."

"Really? How do we not know this?" Rand asked as he moved closer and curled his fingers around hers where they gripped the blanket in a stranglehold.

"It's easy to block it out at home. As long as I can't see it I'm okay."

"I'd close the curtains if there were any," Z said. He rolled to his side and leaned over her. "But maybe I can distract you."

Z slanted his mouth over hers, his lips warm and soft as he nibbled from one corner to the other. She moaned and he took advantage of her parted lips to slide his tongue inside. With gentle sweeps and teasing strokes, he wiped everything from her mind except his tender kisses. Caught up in Z's tantalizing touch, Sunnie gasped when Rand's mouth began nibbling her fingers. Each digit received the same dedicated care before he slowly made his way up her arm, pushing her sleeve up as he went. He nipped and licked a trail along the delicate skin of her wrist, up to the tender flesh inside her elbow. Goose bumps sprang up and a shiver rippled over her from head to toe, but it had nothing to do with fear.

She forgot all about the storm outside. Her attention was held completely by the two men lavishing her body with lush kisses and soothing strokes. They pulled her into a decadent world where only the three of them existed. Hands glided over flesh hidden beneath clothes, each slide a heart-stopping brush of comfort. Arousal simmered, flowed over her like warm water and filled her with contentment. As they continued to assault her body with easy touches, Sunnie slipped into such a relaxed state that her anxiety of the last few hours melted away.

Rand's mouth found her neck, his teeth scraping over her chin. Z pulled his mouth from hers and worked his way across her cheek to her ear where he licked at her lobe, toying with the soft flesh before sucking it between his lips and nipping it with his teeth. Sunnie reached out, her fingers touching hot, hard muscle beneath thin cloth. Both wore T-shirts and she took her time, her fingers exploring their glorious bodies. With every touch, every kiss, Sunnie's concerns slipped away until the only thing that mattered was loving these men. Being loved by them.

Their movements slowed, their kisses turning to soft pecks as they settled into a comfortable embrace. Bracketed between Rand and Z, Sunnie couldn't deny the rightness of the three of them together. She couldn't guarantee fear wouldn't grab hold of her again or that she wouldn't screw up due to her insecurities, but she could promise—to herself if not them—to not let her doubts get the better of her. From now on she'd open her mind, as well as her heart, to all they could have together. With her concerns eased and the guys surrounding her with their warmth it wasn't long before she slipped into sleep.

RAND GAZED down at a sleeping Sunnie. On the other side of her, Z snored softly. The last twenty-four hours had proven exhausting for all of them. Neither of his friends had lasted long after they'd snuggled under the blankets. Their simple touches and kisses had soothed Sunnie's fears and she'd finally relaxed before drifting off, with Z right behind her. But Rand couldn't sleep. Couldn't switch off his mind no matter how hard he tired. He'd known these two were a big part of his life, only he hadn't realized how big until now. If they couldn't make this work, if they screwed up the friendship they'd built over a lifetime, Rand wasn't sure how he'd cope. Or if he even could.

With a sigh, he sank back against the pillow and stared at the ceiling. When he'd suggested they take their friendship further he never imagined the complicated emotions involved. Never once considered that what he'd felt for his two friends could be more. So much more. He and Z had always been close, closer than brothers in many ways, but their connection went deeper than that. If he had to put a name to it, Rand would have to say he loved Zeke Nolan. While there was no physical desire between them, he loved Z in every other way one would for the person they wanted to spend their life with. And wasn't that a kicker?

If someone had told him he'd be fearful of losing the love of his best friend before today, he would have laughed. Rand honestly hadn't known the depth of his feelings for Z or how tangled they were with how he felt about Sunnie. He wasn't sure if he could explain it, this bone-deep love that had built over the years. It wasn't new. Without him noticing, the two people beside him had woven their way not only around his heart, but through his soul and the very fabric of his life. The knowledge had been there all along, but he'd never recognized it. Why would he, when they were so much a part of him and his everyday life that he didn't think of them as separate from himself?

Next to him, Sunnie stirred. She rolled over and curled into his side. The press of her body against his didn't fail to snag his attention. His cock swelled within the confines of his pants. They'd crawled into bed fully clothed and, while he wasn't uncomfortable, he wasn't exactly at ease either, especially now that his libido was taking notice of the woman plastered to him. He drew in a breath and her scent filled his nose, reminding him of the taste of her skin. Rand tried to ignore his growing arousal, but he couldn't resist sliding his arm under her and pulling her closer.

"Can't sleep?"

Her husky voice pulled him from his thoughts. "Sorry, didn't mean to wake you."

"It's okay." Sunnie placed her hand on his chest, her fingers splayed over his heart. "What's wrong?"

"What makes you think anything's wrong?"

"You get insomnia when you worry about things."

She knew him so well. They may not have shared a bed before, but they'd been close in every other way. He sighed. "I never expected it to be so much."

Her body went rigid beside him. "Too much?"

"No. Not that." Rand turned so they were face-to-face. He brushed the hair from her forehead with his fingertips. "I just never knew the depth of our friendship or mine with Z. I'm a little shocked and embarrassed to admit I never realized how much you're both a part of me—how deeply connected we *all* are." He glanced over at where Z slept.

"I know." She smiled. "It's like it was always there, waiting for us to find."

"Yeah." He ran his fingers down her cheek. "I think getting naked has stripped bare more than our bodies."

"I don't want to screw this up, Brandon." Moisture filled her eyes and she blinked rapidly. "I can't lose either of you."

"You won't."

"You can't guarantee that."

"No, I guess not, but I can guarantee I'll do everything I can to make this work." He leaned forward, pressed his lips to hers in a quick kiss. "We can make this work, Sunshine, for all of us."

"I'll second that." Z rolled over and spooned against Sunnie's back. "If we really want this—and I do, more than anything I've ever wanted—then I have absolutely no doubt we'll make it work."

"I don't know how to do this," Sunnie said. "Every relationship I've ever had has been dysfunctional in some way or blown up in my face. I don't want that for us."

"The odds are in our favor." Z sat up and rested his chin on Sunnie's arm. "There's three of us fighting for the same thing."

"But that means three different opinions. Three different perspectives. Three times the chance we'll disagree on something," Sunnie said.

"Three times the love." Sunnie opened her mouth, and Rand placed his fingers over her lips before she could protest further. "I'm not saying we'll agree on everything, but look at us now. We're all in agreement about what we want, and as long as we keep that in sight I think we stand a better than average chance of making it."

"Instead of worrying about what might happen, let's take it one day at a time. Enjoy each moment we have and attack any problems as they arise," Z said.

"How about it, Sunshine? Are you game?" Rand asked.

She took a moment and Rand held his breath. Waited for her to accept what he and Z offered. He didn't really doubt she would, but those few seconds before she answered were the longest in his life. She nodded. Air rushed from his lungs as relief surged through him. But Rand wanted things to be clear right from the start.

"So we agree we're going to pursue a permanent relationship between the three of us?"

"You bet," Z answered.

Sunnie nodded.

"Not good enough, Sunshine." Rand tapped her nose with his fingertip. "Say it."

"Yes."

Rand smiled, his lips stretching farther and farther until his cheeks hurt. "Great. Now let's get some sleep. We've got plans to make tomorrow."

"Plans?" Sunnie asked.

"Well, first we'll have to buy a bigger bed." Z grinned. "Sleeping in this one is no trouble, but none of us has a king at home."

"Z's right. First order of the day is purchasing new bedroom furniture and possibly thinking about renovating the house to accommodate the three of us sharing a room," Rand added.

"Oh. I just thought we'd still have separate rooms."

Rand could see fear in Sunnie's eyes. "Don't panic. We won't rush into anything except the bed. I've been meaning to get a new one anyway. The rest can wait."

Z slid his arm around Sunnie's waist and hugged her from behind, his hand encircling the arm Rand already had draped over her. "Sounds like a plan, but right now all I want to do is hold you both close and go to sleep," Z said.

His friend yawned and Rand soon followed. Leaning over, he kissed Sunnie's forehead. "I'm with Z. Time for sleep."

Sunnie closed her eyes and whispered, "Thank you."

"What for?" Rand asked.

"Not giving up on me."

Rand smiled. "Sunshine, I couldn't walk away from this—from us—if someone had a gun to my head. I've never felt anything as right as being with you and Z."

"Ditto." Z kissed her shoulder. "Now sleep. We get to go shopping with Rand's credit card tomorrow."

She smiled. "Nothing better than spending someone else's money."

He chuckled. "I might be paying for the bed, but Z is buying the hundred percent silk sheets."

"Fine, but no pink and no flowers," Z said.

Sunnie laughed. The robust, genuine sound was music to Rand's ears.

LAUGHING SO HARD her sides ached, Sunnie climbed into the back of Z's car as the guys slipped into the front and shut the doors. Laughter filled the interior while they buckled seat belts and Z started the engine. She glanced out the rear window to see if the saleslady was still watching them, but they'd parked well away from the front of the store and the woman would need to come out of the shop to see them.

"Oh my God, did you see the look on her face?" Rand asked through his laughter.

"Her face turned so red I thought she'd had a stroke." Z choked back his own laughter.

Catching her breath, Sunnie said, "What did you expect when you insisted we all test the mattress for comfort?"

Rand turned to look at her. "We'll all be sleeping on it so we have to agree on which one we get."

Sunnie slumped back against the seat. "I had no idea there were so many mattresses to choose from. I'll admit I'm looking forward to sleeping on it though. Damn, that padded top felt good."

"Fucking amazing is a better description." Z looked over his shoulder and reversed out of the parking spot. "Lucky for us they have one at the warehouse so we only have to wait one night before we get to enjoy it."

"I'll get the new bedding washed when we get home so it's ready to put on tomorrow." Sunnie thought about the quilt, cover, and sheets they'd stashed in the trunk.

They'd picked a striking navy blue with white stripes for the quilt cover and pale blue sheets, not silk like Rand suggested, but the cotton was so soft she couldn't wait to curl up beneath the quilt and feel the fabric slide against her skin. A shiver skittered down her spine at the thought of diving under the covers with Rand and Z. It wasn't the first time arousal had surfaced today, but they'd had so much fun shopping for their new bed that the tension hadn't drawn too tight. Sunnie had been able to forget her fears and enjoy their time together.

Turning to look out the side window, Sunnie watched the scenery go by with little interest. Instead she thought about how good the day had been. How, even though she feared it would be awkward shopping for such an intimate piece of furniture, it had been anything but. Their likes were so similar they hadn't argued about any of their choices. In fact, when they entered the store they all zeroed in on the bedding immediately. The blue-and-white set, on prominent display right inside the front doors, had drawn each of them over, their fingers brushing over the soft material. Sunnie remembered laughing with relief at their mutual appreciation.

They'd collected their bedding choice and headed for the section where the mattresses and frames were displayed. Z told them not to bother looking at frames as he planned to make them one uniquely theirs, so they concentrated on the mattress and base set. Sunnie had giggled as Z went from bed to bed, bouncing on them to test their sturdiness. Rand frowned, but followed along behind him. They spent ages testing each one, making her climb on in the middle while they stretched out on either side to determine which one suited them best. When the saleswoman finally came over their decision had been made.

Sunnie thought she'd die of embarrassment when Rand and Z started discussing the merits of the mattress with the saleswoman. They made no secret of the fact the three of them would be sharing the bed. Once she noticed the woman was far more uncomfortable with the situation than herself, Sunnie couldn't help but smile and enjoy the guys' silliness. She was sure they played it up to make the poor woman turn even redder and, by the time Rand had signed the last of the paperwork for delivery of the bed, Sunnie had no choice but to walk away or risk laughing in the woman's face.

Z turned into their driveway and pushed the remote control to open the roller door. With a smile on her lips, Sunnie waited for him to pull into the garage. When he stopped and put the car in park she frowned and wondered what was wrong. Rand's quietly uttered *fuck* made her insides churn, but that was nothing compared to the heavy ball of dread that fell to the pit of her stomach when she heard her mother's shriek.

"Sunshine Michaels!"

Cold sweat broke out on Sunnie's skin as the immaculately dressed Phoebe Michaels came running down the front steps. Sunnie unbuckled her seat belt and scrambled out of the car. "What? What's wrong?"

"How could you?" Her mother gripped her forearms and shook before dragging Sunnie toward the road. "You know how horrible my life has been. How those bastards took advantage of me and left me to pick up the pieces."

"What?" Sunnie had no idea what her mother was carrying

on about. She dug in her heels and halted Phoebe's mad dash. "Stop, Mother. I haven't a clue what you're talking about."

Phoebe turned, her eyes filled with tears and her cheeks streaked with wet tracks as she looked Sunnie up and down. "I hoped they wouldn't do this to me. Hoped they wouldn't destroy my life completely by corrupting you to their way of thinking."

"What *are* you talking about?" Sunnie finally managed to pull free of her mother's grasp.

"You." Phoebe pointed in Rand and Z's direction. "Them. Your fathers."

Sunnie shook her head. "I don't understand."

"You and these two." Phoebe waved her hand over Sunnie's shoulder, her mouth pinched in disgust. "They're perverted, just like your fathers. I prayed this wouldn't happen. Hoped you'd be normal, but they couldn't even let me have that. They had to take away every last shred of my happiness."

"I don't know what you're talking—"

"Of course you do. It's written all over your face. I can see it in your eyes and the smug smile on your lips. Not to mention the knowing grins on their faces." Phoebe again waved a hand in Rand and Z's direction. "You're fucking both of them and screwing up my life at the same time."

Phoebe burst into tears. Gut-wrenching sobs that doubled her over and Sunnie was at a loss as to what to do. Sunnie began to understand what her mother was talking about and a knot twisted tight in her stomach as she realized their secret was out. Her mother continued to sob and curse. She'd never had a physically demonstrative relationship with her mother, but watching Phoebe cry her eyes out had Sunnie stepping forward and wrapping her arm around her.

"Shh, it's okay." Sunnie didn't know what to think of her

mother's meltdown, never mind the guilt her mother's words made her feel.

"No it's not," Phoebe wailed. "My daughter is a freak just like *them*."

Sunnie stiffened. *A freak?* Memories of childhood taunts flooded her mind. She glanced over her shoulder at Rand and Z, only feet away, and remembered all they'd done in bed together. Bile rose in her throat.

"What will people say?" Phoebe wailed. "You'll lose your job when the school finds out."

Oh God! Her mother was right. How could she possibly believe it was okay to be with both of them? Z made a move toward her and Sunnie shook her head. She needed to think, needed to get out of here, take her hysterically ranting mother home and figure out what to do now. One thing was certain. Phoebe might be screwed up in many ways, but she was right about this. Her mother knew from experience there was nothing normal about being involved with more than one man.

"Come on, Mother, where are your keys? I'll drive you home." Sunnie ushered her mother toward the street and the sexy little convertible parked at the curb. The car was new, but she'd worry about where her mother got the money for this latest extravagance after she'd put some distance between herself and the two men standing in the driveway behind her.

"Yes, yes, take me home." Phoebe sniffled around her tears. "I need to lie down. My life is destroyed. How could you ruin my life like them?"

"Sunnie?"

Rand's question made her feet falter, but she didn't stop. She couldn't face them, couldn't prevent the need to flee taking over, so she raised her voice and kept walking. "I'm taking my mother home."

"Do you want one of us to come pick you up?" Z asked behind her.

Sunnie didn't answer. She quickly bundled her mother into the passenger seat and raced around to the driver's side. Opening the door, she slid into the seat and, sticking the key in the ignition, she fired the engine with a roar then shifted the gear lever into drive. After a brief glance in the side mirror she tore away from the curb and headed down the street as fast as she dared. It took willpower she didn't know she possessed to avoid looking in the rearview mirror.

RAND HUNG up the phone and breathed easier for the first time in more than twenty-four hours. Graham Carter promised he'd find Sunnie. If anyone could find where Phoebe had moved, it was Sunnie's father. Out of the three men who'd raised Sunnie, Graham was the one Phoebe clung to the most. The fact the man had money didn't escape Rand's notice, but right now he didn't care why Sunnie's mother chose to keep Graham abreast of her every move. He just needed to know Sunnie was okay.

"Was that Sunnie?" Z asked as he came into the kitchen.

"No. Graham."

"Graham?" Z's forehead wrinkled before his eyebrows shot up. "You didn't?"

"I had to. I can't stand not knowing where she is or if she's all right."

"Jesus."

"All I did was ask him to find out she's okay." Rand swallowed. "I can't sit here and do nothing. I *need* to know she's safe."

"I get that." Z pulled a beer from the fridge and mumbled,

"I checked today's paper for any reports of local car accidents yesterday."

Rand chuckled. "Glad I'm not the only one going out of his mind with worry."

"No, you're not alone, but Sunnie's gonna be pissed that you brought Graham into this."

"I know, but what choice did we have when her phone is going straight to voice mail?"

Z cracked the top of his beer as the doorbell rang. "Sunnie?"

"Why would she ring the doorbell? She's got keys." Rand pushed back his chair and stood.

"Yeah, but they're in the handbag she left in my car." Z tipped the beer bottle to his mouth.

"Good thing her phone was in her pocket and not her bag," Rand said.

"Fat lot of good that does when she's not answering the damn thing."

"At least she can call us if she wants or needs to."

"Which is why the phone's silence is pissing me off." Z took another swig from his bottle.

Rand understood where his friend was coming from. The longer they went without hearing from Sunnie the more Rand's insides twisted and his chest ached. Her lack of communication made him feel equal parts frustrated, angry, and depressed. And out of control. He hated being out of control. There was nothing he could say that would make either of them feel better so he didn't bother opening his mouth.

He walked from the room and headed down the hallway as the bell rang again, followed by a fist banging on the door.

"Hold your horses, I'm coming," he yelled.

When he reached the front door he yanked it open with a

forced smile plastered to his face. The second he saw who it was, his gut clenched and the smile turned to a grimace.

"Brandon Davis?" A man in a shirt embroidered with the furniture shop's name on the breast pocket stood on the doorstep.

"Yeah, that's me."

"Sign here, please." The guy thrust a clipboard at him.

Rand took the board and used the attached pen to scrawl his signature on the dotted line before handing the paperwork back. Another man opened the back of the truck that had reversed into the driveway. Propping the front door open with his foot, Rand turned to yell down the hallway for Z only to come face-to-face with his best friend.

"The bed's here," Z said.

"Fuck," Rand sighed.

They watched the two men wrestle the base out of the truck. If he'd been in a better mood he might have offered to help, but Rand couldn't bring himself to dredge up any enthusiasm for the delivery. When he'd set up the time it was so they'd all be there. Now he wished they hadn't been so lucky to get one delivered this quickly. All he had to do was direct the men to his room but even that seemed too difficult. He'd dismantled his old bed when he'd gotten home, and each bolt reminded him of the fact Sunnie wasn't here. It was what finally made him ring Graham. As the men approached the front door he left Z to hold it open and led the way down the hall.

After the men had gone, Rand couldn't bring himself to make the new bed even though they had all the sheets washed and ready. Turning on his heel, he headed to the kitchen where Z was cooking dinner. He wasn't hungry but he knew he needed to eat, so he sat at the table and forced himself to consume some of the curry. Each mouthful stuck in his throat and sat heavy in his stomach. Rand pushed his almost untouched plate aside.

"I can't eat."

Z looked up from where he was twirling food around with his fork. "Me either."

Rand's phone chirped signaling a text message, and he shoved his chair back so hard it toppled over, crashing to the floor. Bounding across the room, he snatched the device off the counter and pressed buttons until the message appeared on the screen.

"Who is it?" Z asked.

"I found her."

"What?"

"That's all he says," Rand answered.

"Who? Graham?"

"Yeah." Rand took his eyes off the phone to look at his friend. "He'd have said if she was hurt, right?"

Z nodded. "I'd think so. Are you going to reply?"

"What should I say?"

"That we love her and want her to come home."

"You don't think that's putting pressure on her?" Rand asked.

Z sighed and leaned back in his chair. "Probably. At least get him to tell her we love her. No expectations. Just let her know we're here when she's ready."

"How about..." Rand started pressing buttons. "Tell Sunnie we love her and will wait until she's ready to talk?" He glanced up at Z.

"And that's not pressuring her?"

"Okay, okay." He held the delete button. "I'll remove the second part."

"So, 'tell her we love her'?"

"Yep." Rand hit Send.

"Now what?" Z asked.

Rand shrugged. "We keep waiting."

"Shit!" Z slid his chair back and stood. Grabbing his plate, he headed to the sink.

Rand followed. In silence, they packed away the leftovers and loaded the dishwasher. When they were done they wandered into the living room, but neither could settle and if Rand's own fidgeting hadn't got on his nerves, Z's would have. He stared at the television while Z flicked through channels for the millionth time, never stopping long enough to see a full minute, and Rand couldn't stand it any longer. He pushed to his feet.

"I'm going to shower. Maybe that'll help." He walked from the room as though the hounds of hell were on his ass.

He found no solace in the shower, plagued by memories of what had occurred in there mere days ago. When Rand stepped from beneath the hot spray, his shoulders and back were still rigid with tension. He dried off and wrapped the towel around his hips. Running his fingers through his damp hair, he left the bathroom and found himself in Sunnie's room, staring at her bed. It hadn't been slept in last night and, by the look of things, would remain empty again tonight. Needing to be close to her, he sat on the edge of the mattress and smoothed his palm over her pillow.

Before he could stop himself, he snatched the pillow from the bed and cradled it against his chest, his face buried in the plush padding. Sunnie's scent surrounded him, the soft fragrance one she always wore. Rand didn't know if it was a perfume or body lotion, but he would always associate the smell with Sunnie. It reminded him of summer rain. Clean and fresh. He laid the pillow down and, lifting his legs, stretched out on her bed. Staring at the ceiling, Rand thought about what he'd told Graham. He'd left nothing out, including that the three of them had taken their friendship to a more intimate level.

Every screeched word Phoebe uttered was etched on his brain. The woman had a knack of turning a situation around to being about her. In her mad ramblings yesterday she'd basically accused Sunnie of wrecking her life—not Sunnie's, *hers*. Rand had never liked Phoebe Michaels. Banishing thoughts of that harpy from his mind, he closed his eyes and breathed deep, pulling Sunnie's scent into his lungs. The familiar smell went a long way to soothing his ragged nerves and turbulent thoughts.

Z PULLED on his boxers and left the bathroom to look for Rand. He hadn't seen him in over an hour and it wasn't like his best friend not to say good night. The door to Rand's room was wide open, the new bed unmade and vacant. Bypassing his own room, Z went out into the living room only to find it exactly the way he'd left it before showering. Checking all the windows and doors were locked as he went, Z searched the house before heading to the only two rooms left—his and Sunnie's.

As expected, his bedroom was empty, but Sunnie's was another story. Rand lay sprawled on her bed, his hips barely covered by a towel. And he was snoring loud enough to peel paint. Z smiled. How he hadn't heard Rand before now was a mystery. Glancing at Sunnie's bedside clock, Z accepted that it was unlikely she'd be returning home tonight. Walking around the end of the bed, he climbed onto the other side of the mattress and stretched out with his hands behind his head. He'd take a leaf out of Rand's book and try to find peace in Sunnie's bed even if she wasn't in it.

He couldn't be sure why Sunnie had run. There was no doubt she'd have wanted to calm her mother down, but Z felt she'd used that as an excuse to escape. Just when things had been going well Phoebe had to show up and ruin everything. How Sunnie's mother always managed to be around to pour sadness on the slightest bit of happiness her daughter found—and with such regularity—mystified him and made him think she had some sort of magic powers, or sixth sense at least. She certainly had a flair for making Sunnie believe she didn't deserve to be happy.

"You don't smell like Sunnie."

Z turned his head to look at Rand. "And thank God for that. She smells like flowers."

"For a second there I thought she'd come home."

"Ah, shit, sorry." Z turned back to resume staring at the ceiling. "I didn't think of that. You were snoring loud enough to demolish walls."

"Guess I finally succumbed to exhaustion. Didn't sleep at all last night and work was flat out today."

"I'm not sure I'll be as lucky."

"I take it she hasn't called."

"No. Not a word from her or Graham."

"If there's still nothing in the morning I'll ring Graham again. I think I'll stay home tomorrow. Doubt I'll get any work done at the office," Rand said.

"I brought some plans home with me today. I can work on permits and ordering supplies from here."

"I can't go back," Rand murmured.

"Back?" Z looked at his friend.

"Back the way things were." Rand dragged his hand down his face. "I can't pretend I wasn't buried inside heaven if Sunnie doesn't want to try and make this work."

"Don't think I can either. But let's cross that bridge, when and *if* we get to it."

"I can't help thinking we're already there."

"No. We're standing in sideshow alley watching Phoebe perform. We've been here before. Sunnie will come around. Or Phoebe will get tired of her daughter's attention and move on. Again."

"Damn. I hope Sunnie wises up before that."

"Me too, but history says it's unlikely."

"So we pick up the pieces again."

Z sighed. "Yeah. Like every other time cyclone Phoebe blows through Sunnie's life."

"I don't think Graham was too happy to hear that Phoebe was at it again."

"What did he say?"

"Not much really. Just that he'd put a stop to Phoebe's interference for good."

"Wow. Sounds like I'm not the only one looking to read Sunnie's mother the riot act."

"I'd say there are five of us in that line. Graham said he'd call Roger and Wayne."

"Oh, boy." Z smiled. "Last time the three of them got together Sunnie ended up moving in here in spite of her mother's loud protests."

"I remember. The three of them are a force to be reckoned with."

Z sat up and pulled the cover down so he could crawl underneath. If they were going to spend the night in Sunnie's bed he may as well get comfortable just in case he did manage to fall asleep. He thumped the pillow a couple of times before lying down and pulling the quilt up to his waist.

"Getting comfy, I see," Rand said.

"May as well. Don't see much point in waiting anywhere else."

"Me either." Rand pulled off his towel and slid beneath the covers. "Do you think she'll take the chance?"

"I know it doesn't look like it now, but yeah, I think she will."

"Are you sure that's not just wishful thinking?"

Z chuckled. "There's a good dose of that in there, but I have to go on how things were before Phoebe showed up and that, my friend, was definitely Sunnie taking a chance."

Rand smiled. "Yeah, it was."

"Now we just have to wait out the storm that is Sunnie's mother and then we can get back to working out the new status quo."

"I think we were well on the way to establishing that this weekend."

"We were, but now we have to fit around life. Work, friends, family."

Rand laughed. "Well, we know how one member of Sunnie's family feels about things."

"Phoebe might be Sunnie's mother, but she's not family. How many times has Sunnie spent Christmas or birthdays with her in the years since high school?"

Silence met Z's question. Neither of them seemed to be able to recall when Phoebe had been present.

"Damn. I don't think Sunnie has spent Christmas with her mother since we were teenagers."

"Good thing she has her dads and us."

"You know, now that I think about it, I don't recall Phoebe being around at Sunnie's graduation either."

"No, if I remember right, she was in Bali with her latest sugar daddy when we graduated."

"Christ. She's a real piece of work." Rand looked Z in the eye. "We need to stop her from hurting Sunnie from now on."

"Oh don't worry. I plan to make certain she doesn't hurt her again."

"You can't guarantee that. No one can."

"Maybe not, but I can sure as hell make it difficult for her to get near Sunnie. And I plan on making sure Sunnie knows exactly how much she's loved every day for the rest of my life."

"Ditto."

"She just needs to come home so we can put our plan into action." Z was fairly confident Sunnie would take a chance on loving them both, but he crossed his fingers just in case.

9

SUNNIE FLIPPED through the papers on her mother's desk. She'd only been here once since Phoebe moved in months ago, and curiosity compelled her to snoop around a little. Her mother didn't really include Sunnie in her life. Then again, Phoebe didn't let anyone get too close. Even when Sunnie was a child, Phoebe kept things, *people*, compartmentalized. All in neat little boxes at arm's length. At least that's how it seemed to Sunnie.

Yesterday was a perfect example. The minute they'd walked in the door Phoebe had claimed a headache and taken herself to bed. But not before making Sunnie promise she wouldn't leave. After all, what loving daughter would abandon her mother in her darkest hour? Sunnie knew her mother had manipulated her, but she'd needed the time to think. To consider her next move—rehash the ones she'd already made. Being alone the entire night had given Sunnie plenty of time to reflect.

By the time morning rolled around Sunnie had come to a decision, one that meant possibly destroying the fragile relationship she had with her mother. But she couldn't deny she was in love with Rand and Z. Would never forgive herself if she didn't try to make a deeper relationship work with them. Of course the minute Phoebe had emerged from her bedroom Sunnie's plans were put on hold. Her mother was in desperate need of help and what self-respecting daughter wouldn't be there for her mother?

Spending the day with her mother had been an eye-opener. She'd never considered Phoebe as anything other than her mother, but after hours of shopping and salon visits Sunnie began to see the woman behind the mother label. And she didn't like her. Phoebe was manipulative, petulant, selfish, and downright nasty. She hated to admit that her mother had fewer manners than the five- and six-year-olds Sunnie taught, but there was no use pretending, and she doubted Phoebe would appreciate it if she did.

Their last appointment of the day had been with a hairdresser and manicurist. It seemed Phoebe had a date. Sunnie hadn't met the new man in her mother's life, and judging by the way Phoebe hustled out the front door when the bell rang, she wasn't going to. She glanced at the wall clock. Almost an hour since her mother left and she still hadn't called a taxi to take her home. Her mother had given her a handful of cash, told her to order pizza, and not wait up. Only Sunnie had no intention of staying another night.

She needed to go home. Wanted to with a sudden urgency that had her quick-stepping across the living room to the phone. As she picked up the handset the doorbell chimed. The melodic rhythm of some classical tune filled the house. Sunnie hurried into the foyer. Reaching the door, she bent to look through the peephole. Even distorted by the miniature lens, Graham Carter was an intimidating presence. Straightening, Sunnie slipped the safety chain free and turned the deadbolt.

As the door opened she had to jump back to avoid being smacked in the face as her fathers rushed in. She wasn't prepared for the other two men flanking Graham and her stomach dropped to her toes at the sight of Roger and Wayne on either side of him.

"What's wrong?" Her gaze darted between the three men.

"Is Phoebe here?" Graham asked.

"No. You missed her."

"We're not here to see her, Sunshine," Roger said.

"Then—"

"Consider this an intervention," Wayne added.

"Intervention?" She shook her head. "What for? Me?"

"Yes." Graham gripped her elbow and guided her out the door.

"Wait. Where are we going?" Sunnie glanced over her shoulder to see Wayne shutting the front door.

"To dinner." Roger led the way down Phoebe's path to the car parked at the curb, where he opened the rear door and waited for her to climb in. "Slide all the way over. I'm jumping in the back with you."

Sunnie scooted along the leather seat to make room. She buckled her seat belt and a wave of nostalgia flow over her. When she was little they'd pick her up together whenever her mother deemed they were allowed to see her. Usually the visits with her fathers coincided with a new boyfriend for Phoebe. Smiling, she thought it ironic that some things never changed.

"Hey, you remember that little pizza place we used to take you to?" Wayne asked as he sank into the front passenger seat.

"Yes." More happy memories filled Sunnie's mind. "Are we going there?"

"Yep." Graham started the car. "Nothing but the best for our number-one girl."

Sunnie grinned as the engine revved and Graham steered

the car out onto the road. "So what kind of intervention are you doing?"

"No talking until we get to Mamma's." Roger patted her knee.

"None at all?"

"Well you could tell us how handsome we are." Wayne glanced at her over his shoulder. "Never hurts to hear."

Sunnie laughed. "You don't need me to tell you that. What about all those women you're always dating? Surely they're enough to boost your ego."

"Nobody boosts the ego like your number-one girl." Roger leaned over and kissed Sunnie's cheek.

Her heart jolted. They all called her their number-one girl but no one knew that for sure. She didn't understand how these three men could accept her as their own as well as each other's. "How do you do that?"

"Do what, Sunshine?" Graham asked.

"Love me like a father when you know it's possible you aren't?" She really needed to understand. If she hoped to have a life with Rand and Z then she could expect to come up against this very thing in the future.

"We're almost there. We'll talk over Mamma's all-meat special." Graham turned into the parking lot beside Mamma's.

Roger gripped her hand and gave it a squeeze. "Come on. Things are never as bad as they seem."

"How can you say that when you have no idea what's going on?"

Roger's gaze darted to Wayne then Graham.

"Oh my God! They told you!" Sunnie's cheeks burned with embarrassment.

Graham leaned between the front seats and cupped her chin, lifting her face until their eyes met. "Yes, but they're both going out of their mind with worry, Sunshine. Why didn't you call them to say you were okay?"

Sunnie had picked up her phone to do just that a hundred times during the last twenty-four hours, but each time she did her mother's voice screeching *freak* echoed in her head and she couldn't bring herself to press the buttons. She closed her eyes and leaned into her father's touch.

"I wanted to, but Mother..."

"Yes, I can imagine what Phoebe would have to say about it." Wayne flung his door open and climbed out of the car. Bending down, he ducked his head back inside. "Come on, I'm starving and I'm not talking about that woman on an empty stomach."

The car shook when Wayne slammed the door.

"Hey. Watch the car." Graham opened his door and got out.

"Let's go, Sunshine." Roger pulled her across the backseat behind him as he got out. "You'll have to excuse Wayne. He's tried to get us to set you straight about Phoebe for years."

"Set me straight?" She walked beside Roger, her pace matching his.

"There are some things you need to know about your mother."

"What sort of things?" Sunnie stopped at the front door of the pizzeria.

Roger pressed his hand to the base of her spine and nudged her inside. "Dinner first."

Sunnie didn't get to protest because Roger slid his arm around her shoulders and ushered her to a booth in the back. He nudged her onto the bench seat and followed her. Graham and Wayne took the bench across from them. Questions buzzed in her head and she wanted to get right into the topic, but the waitress came over to take their order. Once the woman had jotted down what they wanted and disappeared, Sunnie dived right in to the reason they were there.

"Okay, no more avoiding. What gives?"

"First let me say I've spoken to Brandon and we know everything up until the point where you left with your mother yesterday," Graham said.

"Everything?" Sunnie chewed on her bottom lip.

Graham nodded.

"Oh." She sucked in a breath. Heat surged over her chest and up her throat until it burned her cheeks. Sunnie ducked her head.

Roger placed a finger under her chin and tipped her face up. "You have no reason to hide, Sunshine. Never be ashamed of loving someone."

Before Sunnie could think of anything to say, the waitress returned with their drinks. The interruption gave her time to take a deep breath, and a second one as the drinks were handed out. Although she didn't feel one hundred percent comfortable talking about her love life with her fathers, she knew she had to. Especially her fears. As the waitress walked away the words came tumbling out.

"I've always loved them."

"I know." Graham's hand curled over hers. "But you've never allowed yourself to be in love with them before. What changed?"

"I don't know. One second we're friends—housemates—and the next we're getting it on in the kitchen." Sunnie's face flamed with her confession. She hadn't meant to reveal so much.

Roger chuckled. "Nothing wrong with a little heat in the kitchen."

"Roger!"

Roger sighed. "You know I preferred it when you were little and called me Dad."

Sunnie sat back, stunned at Roger's admission. "But Phoebe said—"

"Do not take anything Phoebe says into account, Sunshine. That woman lies more than she breathes." Wayne's hand clenched into a fist where it rested on the table.

Graham squeezed her hand beneath his to get her attention. "Your mother told you to stop calling us Dad?"

She nodded.

"Bitch!" Wayne's voice vibrated with anger.

"Wayne," Graham cautioned. "Sunshine, it's time we told you some things. Maybe then you can make decisions about your life without your mother's influence."

"Funny. Phoebe said something similar about you three," Sunnie said.

"I'm not surprised." Roger picked at the label on his beer. "Why did you run, Sunshine?"

Sunnie couldn't answer. Her mouth had gone dry and the lump in her throat blocked all words. But if she wanted to keep their respect—and her own—she had to be honest. She took a sip of her Coke. The sweet icy liquid fizzed on her tongue, bubbled as she swallowed. After a couple of gulps she licked her lips and spoke.

"I panicked. I'm not proud of it and I can't say it was rational. No, actually, I can say with honesty it was completely irrational, but Phoebe was crying and saying I was a freak like all of you. What really got to me was she'd already done what I was attempting and failed. I couldn't get past that."

"Phoebe has never done what you're contemplating," Graham said.

"Of course she has. She tried to have a relationship with the three of you."

"No." Roger grabbed her free hand. "Phoebe never loved any of us. And she never once wanted to have all of us in her life. She played us, Sunshine. Plain and simple, she used each of us to get what she wanted only she got trapped in her own web when she fell pregnant with you."

"What? But I thought... Phoebe said—"

"She lied," Wayne growled. "We knew she was seeing all of us. And we let her. I can't speak for Graham or Roger, but I was in love with Phoebe, or who I thought she was anyway. It didn't take long after she told us she was pregnant for me to fall out of love with her."

"Here, I want you to see something." Roger pulled his wallet from his pocket and removed a photo. He placed it on the table in front of her. "See that?"

"Yes, it's us, at a carnival. I was six." Sunnie stared at the picture as memories assailed her.

"Rose took it, remember?" Roger brushed his index finger over the image of a younger Sunnie. "This was the week after Rose and I found out we couldn't have kids. Or more importantly, *I* can't have them."

Her gaze darted up to meet Roger's. "What? But that means..."

"I can't be your biological father."

"Then why?"

"Look at the picture, Sunshine," Graham directed. "What do you see?"

"Us."

"No." He tapped the table next to the photo. "Look closer. What is it about these four people stands out?"

Sunnie studied the image of three grown men laughing with a small blonde girl twirling between them. Every second of that night was etched in her memory with permanent ink. They'd treated her to every ride, every game, every stick of cotton candy she could eat. Anything her heart desired was hers. Sunnie sucked in a breath. She could see it. In their faces. On hers.

"You love me."

"Yes." Roger wove his fingers through hers. "I may not have been responsible for your genetic makeup, but I'm your father in every way that counts."

Sunnie couldn't take her eyes off the man who'd taken on the role of father when he didn't have to.

"We talked about it." He used his hand to indicate Graham and Wayne. "Us—Rose. We knew no matter what, none of us could bear to lose you. Rose and I couldn't love you more if you were made from our flesh and blood because we've got something better, Sunshine. Love. A love so great it takes my breath."

"But why would Phoebe do that? Why would she say you could be my father if there was no possibility?"

"She doesn't know. She'd already made all our lives miserable when Rose and I got married. We didn't want her to have something else she could use against us. Or you," Roger explained.

"After Roger discovered his situation," Graham said, "Wayne and I decided to find out which of us was your father. Phoebe would never allow us to have a DNA test done without dragging it through the courts and making all our lives hell. So we did something I'm not proud of, but I'd do again in a heartbeat."

Sunnie stared at the man she'd considered her father regardless of their unorthodox circumstances. "What did you do?" she whispered.

Wayne smiled. "I've got a close friend who's a doctor. He helped us get a sample. It was painless and you thought you were just having a regular checkup."

Silence descended. Sunnie waited for them to tell her who her biological father was, but no one spoke.

"Well?" Graham asked.

"Well what?"

"Aren't you mad at us for what we did?" Wayne asked.

"No, why would I be?" Sunnie glanced between all three of them. "We all had a right to know and Phoebe certainly wasn't going to tell."

"Yeah, the results gave us a little insight into why she refused to admit who was responsible," Roger murmured.

"What do you mean?" Sunnie's stomach clenched. The looks on their faces made her think she wouldn't like the answer.

"Phoebe lied." Wayne thumped his fist against the table. "Always a lie."

A shiver snaked down her spine. "Tell me."

"None of us are your biological father," Graham said.

Sunnie was dumbfounded. "How is that possible?"

"Phoebe was seeing someone else." Roger sighed.

"W-who?" Sunnie's voice shook.

"That's the hard part, Sunshine." Graham speared his fingers through his hair, tugging on the ends. "We don't know. I had a private investigator look into it but came up with nothing concrete. He did discover she'd been seeing a married man around the time you were conceived, but he died about a year after you were born so we didn't pursue it any further."

"If you want we can give you his details or look into it further," Wayne added.

"No." Sunnie didn't want to think about the possibility of someone else being her father.

"Sunshine." Roger tapped the picture still on the table in front of her. "This is what counts. Not genetics."

She smiled warily. "I know."

"We didn't want to make things more complicated. We just want you to make the best decision for you, Brandon, and Zeke," Graham said.

"You can't do that with Phoebe interfering," Roger added.

"What she wants doesn't matter. It never mattered, the only reason we let her get her way all these years was to protect you. She proved time after time she wasn't above using you to make us do her bidding," Wayne explained.

"But you all could have walked away."

Sunnie watched as each of them looked down at Roger's photo and smiled.

"Not in this lifetime, Sunshine." Graham let go of her hand and leaned back. "Here comes our pizza."

The waitress placed the large pan on the stand she'd put on the table earlier. Sunnie reached for a piece but the crust was too hot to touch and she pulled her hand back to blow on her burned fingers.

"Careful." Roger grabbed her wrist and examined her fingertips. "It doesn't look as though you've done any damage."

"I'm fine. Barely a sting." Sunnie tried to pull her hand from his grasp.

"Not yet. Let me kiss it better." He brought her fingers to his mouth and placed a soft peck on the tip of each. "There. All better."

Reminded of days when a simple kiss could right her world made Sunnie's eyes sting with tears. She'd never felt anything other than loved by all three of these men. As a child she'd known every day that they'd hand her the moon if they could. It made her realize she'd let her mother interfere with that. When Sunnie had been old enough to get curious Phoebe had taken advantage by twisting the truth or telling outright lies. It had fractured her relationship with her fathers to the point that she'd legally changed her name at eighteen.

"I'm sorry."

"For what, Sunshine?" Roger asked.

"For letting Phoebe tarnish everything we are. For being blind to what is really important."

"And what's that?" Graham asked.

"Love." Sunnie smiled. "Hanging out with you guys over pizza, and letting you pay the bill."

"Hey, squirt." Roger tweaked the end of Sunnie's nose. "For that we'll do a runner and leave you to wash dishes."

"Bet I'd beat you out the front door if you tried." Sunnie bumped Roger's shoulder with hers. "You're getting old, ya know."

"Watch it or I'll take my pizza and share it with some other little girl," Roger joked.

Sunnie's smile widened at the familiar banter. "I'll sic Rose on you if you try."

"Damn. Foiled by the women I love." Roger sighed dramatically, making Sunnie laugh.

"I've forgotten how much you make me laugh."

"Not much chance to do that lately," Wayne said.

"That's going to change." Sunnie tested the pizza to see if it had cooled enough to hold. "As soon as I fix things with Rand and Z I'm going to organize more outings like this." The budding relationship with Rand and Z wasn't the only one in need of TLC and Sunnie intended to put one hundred percent into improving the bond with all the men in her life.

After they devoured the pizza Graham called the waitress over to order a second one but Sunnie decided she wanted dessert instead. She had a hankering for some gelato. The last time she'd indulged in the yummy Italian treat had been in this very restaurant with her current companions, so she was definitely overdue for some delicious sugary goodness.

"Are you sure you don't want more pizza?" Wayne asked.

"Nope, I'm going to have a double helping of lemon gelato."

"We'll have a small Mamma's all-meat special and a double scoop of lemon gelato," Graham told the waitress.

"Do you want me to bring the gelato when the pizza is ready or now?"

"Oh, now please." Sunnie nudged Roger with her elbow. "Let me out. I wanna run to the bathroom before my dessert comes."

Sunnie returned from the bathroom to find her gelato waiting for her. Only problem was there were three distinct spoonfuls missing.

"Hey." She slid into the booth seat Roger had vacated for her. "I don't remember saying I'd share."

As Roger sat, he did something he hadn't since Sunnie had been a child. He ruffled her hair. The roller coaster of emotions she'd been on in the last few days hit the biggest dip and she couldn't stop the sudden flood of tears.

"Jesus." Roger pulled her into his arms and rocked her.

She had no idea how long she sat, held close in her father's arms, bawling her eyes out. By the time the last tear had dropped Sunnie felt completely wrung out. Sniffing back the final one, she pulled free of Roger's embrace.

"Here." Graham offered her some napkins.

"Sorry."

"Nothing for you to be sorry about, Sunshine." Wayne pushed a glass of water in front of her. "Have a drink to soothe your throat."

"I need to go home."

"We'll take you as soon as you've given yourself time to settle." Graham signaled to get the waitress's attention. "Can we get that pizza to go, thanks?"

"I'll pay the bill and then we can head to my place so you

can freshen up before we take you home." Wayne stood and headed for the counter.

"I should just go home." Her protest sounded weak even to her own ears.

"No." Roger helped her out of the booth. "You need to let your emotions level off first. It won't hurt Brandon and Zeke to wait a little longer."

"Besides, you'll want to try out Wayne's bathroom. You haven't seen what he's done to the apartment either." Graham fell into step next to her.

"He finally got rid of the orange kitchen?"

"Yeah, finally," Roger murmured. "He didn't have much choice. After he bought the whole block he renovated the lot. His place now takes up the entire top floor."

"Wow. I didn't know."

"You've missed a few things over the last few years, Sunshine, but don't panic. We'll be happy to spend hours telling you everything that's gone on." Graham held open the door.

"I'd like that."

"So would we, Sunshine," Roger said as they stepped out into the cool, even air.

Sunnie shivered and Roger tucked her closer against his side, his hand rubbing up and down her arm in an attempt to ward off the chill.

"Come on, let's hustle." Wayne caught up with them. "We need to get our girl home where she belongs."

"Aren't we heading to your place first?" Sunnie asked.

"Sure are. And while we wait for you to get freshened up we'll indulge in some dessert." Wayne held up a plastic bag and jiggled it. "Four servings of lemon gelato."

Slipping into the backseat of Graham's car, Sunnie marveled at how lucky she was. Not one of these men was responsible for bring her into this world, yet they overlooked that major factoid and gave her unconditional love. They'd handled her meltdown with ease and, even though she'd snubbed them over the years, they continued to take care of her. She hoped with all her heart that Rand and Z would prove to be as generous toward any children they might share.

Sunnie choked on her breath. If she hadn't already come to the conclusion that she wanted a relationship with Rand and Z, her last thought would have confirmed it. She wanted children of her own one day, and she wanted them with her two best friends. The question was: did they?

10

SUNNIE USED the spare key she'd given Graham in the lock and pushed the door open. Turning, she waved to let her fathers know she was okay and slipped quietly into the house. It was well after midnight and, even though she'd slept very little in the last few days, she wasn't tired. She shut and locked the door before stepping out of her flip-flops. The dark hallway loomed in front of her but she knew the placement of every piece of furniture in the house so there was no chance she'd stub a toe or bash a shin on her way to finding the two men she'd come home to.

A faint trace of curry lingered on the air and she took a deep breath, disappointed she'd missed one of Z's signature meals. She wasn't sure how he did it, but his curries rivaled the best Indian restaurants in town. Tiptoeing along the hall, Sunnie bypassed the living room and kitchen, and headed straight to the rear of the house and the bedrooms. As she neared Rand's room, she could hear him snoring and a smile tugged at her lips. But when she stood in his doorway, what she saw turned her smile to a frown. A shimmer of moonlight coated the room in an eerie glow. The new bed sat front and center, the mattress unmade and Rand nowhere to be seen.

She could still hear him. The deep, nasally rasps could easily be mistaken for an engine of some kind. Sunnie remembered the first time she'd heard the sound it had scared the life out of her. Now, though, she used that chest-rattling noise to find her man.

Make that men.

Rand and Z were sprawled on her bed. Their muscular bodies made the queen mattress look no bigger than a pillow. She padded over and used their state of slumber to her advantage. Studying each of them, Sunnie cataloged their attributes. From the long legs to the buff chests and chiseled abs, both of them were mighty fine to look at. And look she did. Until the urge to run her tongue along bulging biceps and sink her teeth into tender flesh had her insides tingling and her panties soaking wet.

"Are you planning to crawl into bed or stand there all night?"

"Shit!" Sunnie's gaze snapped up and connected with Rand's. "You scared the life out of me."

"No more than waking to find you standing there like an ax murderer," Rand said.

"I was hoping she was a wet dream getting ready to strip." Z pushed up on his elbows, a cocky grin on his face. His gaze traveled her body from head to toe before meeting hers. "You're a sight for sore eyes, Sunshine."

Sunnie couldn't find any words to say. She'd rehearsed a speech on the way home, but now not one of those words found their way to her tongue. Instead all she could think about was running said tongue over naked skin. Grazing fingertips and nails over rippling muscles as she explored the bare bodies before her.

"Come here, Sunshine." Rand's quietly issued command had her moving before the thought formed.

She knelt on the end of the bed between their legs. Before she got any closer and her hormones took over she needed to tell them why she'd gone. Why she'd come back. But the words stuck in her throat and the only thing that came out was one croaky word.

"Sorry."

"Never apologize for the way you feel." Z sat up, leaned forward and brushed the back of his fingers down her cheek. "It's natural to be frightened. We're going out on a limb here. None of us really knows what we're doing."

"Come up here and lie between us." Rand patted the bed next to him.

"I'm not ready—" As much as she wanted to surrender to the pleasure each of them could give her, Sunnie knew they had to talk first.

"Just talk, Sunshine. All we're going to do is talk." Rand curled his fingers around her wrist and tugged her up the bed.

Relieved, Sunnie spun around and lay on her back, positioning herself between them. Heat radiated off them, causing little swirls of warmth to twist through her. She tried to decide where to start, what to tell them first, and concluded it didn't matter. Tonight would be about opening the door she'd slammed shut yesterday.

"I panicked. I can't say I won't do it again, but I can promise I won't run from you—from us—next time." Sunnie licked her dry lips, tried to swallow past the constriction in her throat. "I love you both. I want this."

"Thank God." Z rolled over until he hovered above her. "You have no idea how sweet those words sound."

She smiled and cupped his face. "I think I do. Saying them

—feeling them—knowing that this emotion is real, is the single most thrilling, and terrifying, experience of my life."

"We'll hold your hands." Rand took her hand as his face came into view beside Z's. "You know I'm petrified we'll screw this up somehow."

"You are?" Sunnie couldn't believe the smooth, sophisticated, in control Brandon Davis would be frightened of anything, let alone her.

Rand bent until his forehead rested on hers. "You terrify me."

"*Me?*"

"Okay, not you exactly, the emotions you provoke. I've never known anything like it and I certainly haven't a clue what to do with them."

"That makes two of us," Z added.

"Three." Sunnie smiled. "I guess we help each other work them out."

"I like that plan," Z said. "But where do we start?"

The next step suddenly clear in her mind, Sunnie pushed them back and scrambled off the bed. "As we intend to go on."

"Where are you going?" Rand's words held the razor edge of panic.

"We should start where we aim to finish." She smiled at them.

"Um...okay, and where is that?" Z asked as he followed her off the bed.

"Together." Sunnie headed out of the room and down the hall, her mind set on her destination.

"Then where the hell are you going?" Rand called behind her.

Sunnie made a beeline for Rand's room and the bed. Flicking on the light as she entered, she searched the room for the new bedding. In typical Rand style, the quilt and sheets were neatly stacked on his chest of drawers. Grabbing the sheet, Sunnie walked to the bed and tossed the cotton fabric over the mattress.

"You're making the bed?" Z asked as he entered the room, Rand right on his heels.

She turned to face them. "We should start where we aim to finish."

They grinned and spoke in unison. "Together."

Sunnie smiled and held out her hands.

RAND WASTED no time getting to the woman he loved. Pulling her close he breathed in her scent and tightened his grip. "I love you."

Sunnie stiffened in his arms but he wasn't about to let her insecurities spoil the moment. He pushed her arm's length away and focused his gaze on hers. "I've always loved you. You know that." He tapped her chest with his hand. "In here, you know."

Z moved in beside them and wove his fingers through her hair. "You just have to stop thinking so hard and feel, Sunshine. Turn off that brain of yours and feel the love we have for you."

Her gaze flicked between them. "I'm terrified this isn't real." She trembled beneath Rand's fingers. "I'm terrified I'll do something to make you stop."

Rand smiled. "If you haven't done that by now it isn't going to happen."

"We've seen you at your worst, Sunshine, we've seen you at your best, and yet here we still are." Z brushed his lips on Sunnie's temple. "Loving you with every breath we take."

"Oh." Her eyes filled with moisture.

"Hey, no tears." Rand brushed a fingertip across her eyelashes. "It rips me up to see you cry, Sunnie."

She smiled. "They're happy tears. Promise."

"In that case, I'm gonna make you cry every day for the rest of our lives," Z said.

Rand looked at his friend. "Shit, Z, really?"

Z stared at him. "What?"

Sunnie's laughter filled the room. "That has to be the most romantic unromantic thing I've ever heard."

A sheepish grin curled Z's mouth. "Hey, what can I say? I have a way with words."

"Oh, yeah, definitely. You have me melting at your feet with that one."

"Melting, huh?" Z moved closer to Sunnie, his body brushing against hers. "Bet Rand and I can make you melt without a word."

"I like the sound of that." Rand crowded into Sunnie's other side, wedging her between them.

She sucked in a breath. "You think I'm going to argue that?"

"No." Rand trailed a finger down her cheek, over her jaw and lower until he tugged on the neckline of her T-shirt. "I think you're going to let us do whatever we want and enjoy every second of it."

Sunnie's eyes dilated and her breathing shallowed. He slipped his hand around and under her right breast to cup the weighty mound in his palm as Z did the same with her left. A moan rolled off her tongue and Rand leaned forward to put his lips on hers. But she surprised him before their mouths could connect by ducking out of their embrace and racing toward the bed.

"Last one on does everyone's washing for a month," she threw over her shoulder as she landed on the bed.

He looked at Z. "You thinking what I'm thinking?"

"Yeah, let's make little Miss Smarty Pants take back those words."

"On three."

"What are you two up to?" Sunnie eyed them warily.

Under his breath Rand counted. "One, two..." He grinned at Z. "Three!"

They pounced. The mattress dipped and sprang back as they landed next to her. Sunnie squealed and tried to scramble out of reach, but they weren't about to let her get away.

Not now.

Not ever.

EPILOGUE

Z TIGHTENED the last nut and shimmied out from behind the bed. He should have waited for Rand so he didn't have to do all the heavy lifting on his own, but he'd wanted to surprise his best friend just as much as Sunnie. Tossing the spanner in his toolbox, he pushed to his feet and admired his handiwork. It had taken six months to carve. Six months of hiding the project from the two people closest to him. He'd lied about working late and that hadn't sat well in his gut, but the end result would be worth it. At least he prayed it would.

He put his weight behind the shove and after the third push the bed slid back against the wall. Straightening the covers and dropping the pillows in place, he admired the finished product and smiled. It was pretty damn impressive even if he said so himself. He'd grab a quick shower and then get dinner started. Z had planned the evening right down to the last detail. Rand and Sunnie would come home from work and he'd have a nice home-cooked meal, along with a decent bottle of wine, waiting. The only glitch in his plan was keeping his two housemates out of their bedroom.

Frowning, he picked up his toolbox and headed for the laundry. It shouldn't be too difficult to distract them and if it wasn't for Sunnie's inability to wait he'd just tell them to stay out of the room until after dinner. He smiled when he remembered trying to keep her out of their new bathroom before it was finished. Rand had wanted to unveil the huge tub big enough for the three of them after the refurb was complete. Only Sunnie couldn't stand to wait, and no matter how much they'd pleaded with her, she'd sneaked in to take a peek.

"Damn woman," he muttered.

"What have I done now?"

Z spun on his heel, the toolbox banging into the side of his leg. "Fuck!"

Sunnie smiled. "Nice."

"What the hell are you doing here?" Why hadn't he heard her come in?

"Um...I live here?" She arched one brow.

"Had enough of us already, Z?" Rand entered the hall from the living room.

"What the hell is going on?" Z demanded. "You two are supposed to be at work."

"We could say the same, Z." Rand motioned to the toolbox in Z's hand. "What gives?"

Before he could answer Sunnie moved closer, invading his personal space and cupping his face in her hands. "You've been distant for months. Working late, disappearing on weekends. If you want out, Z..."

The tears that formed in her eyes just about killed him. "No! Shit no!" He dropped the box to the floor and wrapped his arms around her. "I'm exactly where I want and should be."

"Then what gives, man?" Rand asked as he moved in to bracket Sunnie between them. He placed his hands on Z's shoulders. "You're holding back, Z, and we don't like it."

Fuck! He might have kept his project a secret but he'd obviously not been able to hide it completely. With a sigh, he mentally watched his reveal plan fly out the window. Well, he'd just roll with it. They'd certainly managed to live without a plan so far and, other than this little blip, they'd had a pretty smooth run since they embarked on their three-way relationship.

"It's not what either of you are thinking." He swallowed over his dry throat. God, he hoped they liked what he'd done. "I have been hiding something, but it's a good something, and if you two could have just waited a few more hours..." No point dwelling on that, though.

He pulled back and grabbed one of Sunnie's hands. It seemed strange, but Z didn't let that stop him from taking Rand's hand as well. Rather than explain he towed them behind him down the hall and into their room.

"Oh my." Sunnie tugged her hand from his and walked over to the bed.

"Wow." Rand followed her.

Z waited by the door, his shoulders stiff, his spine straight and the churning in his gut threatening to expel his lunch. Sunnie ran her hand over the smooth corner post before turning back to him with tears in her eyes. His gut clenched. God, he hoped they were happy tears.

"Z." She ran at him then. From two feet away she launched herself into his arms. "I never thought... God! What I thought."

"Shh..." Z's gaze connected with Rand's. "I'm sorry I worried you. I wanted it to be a surprise."

"Well, it certainly is that." Rand turned back to the headboard. "I can't get over the detail in this thing. It must have taken months."

Z laughed. "Six. But if we're counting hours it wasn't that

long." He walked over and sat on the bed, Sunnie still in his arms.

"Jesus. Sunnie, you have to see this." Rand cupped the back of her head. "He's carved you in here."

Her head snapped up, barely missing Z's chin. "What?" She scrambled off his lap and over to where Rand was pointing. "Holy shit!"

"We're all in it." Z shrugged. "It's our bed so I thought we should all be part of it."

Sunnie trailed her fingertips over the surfer riding a wave. "Tell me."

Z moved over behind her and pointed to where he'd carved the image of himself into the timber. "I'm there, on the sand, ready to hit the waves. That's Rand." He indicated the rider high on the crest of a wave. "And you, lying under the summer sun."

"Damn." Rand clapped Z on the shoulder. "You nailed us."

He laughed. "The three most important things in our lives."

Rand smiled. "Sand, surf, and Sunnie."

ABOUT THE AUTHOR

Rhian Cahill is the alter ego of a former stay-at-home mother of four. With motherly duties rapidly dwindling Rhian is able to make use of the fertile imagination she used to keep herself sane for all those years of slavery. Having spent years living overseas and visiting tropical climates has helped inspire some steamy stories.

Multi-published in erotic romance and contemporary romance, Rhian, with the help of Mr. Muse, spends her days and nights writing.

When not glued to the keyboard you'll find her book or knitting in hand avoiding any and all housework as much as possible.

For more on Rhian –

Website – http://www.rhiancahill.com/
Newsletter signup – http://www.rhiancahill.com/contact/newsletter/
Twitter – https://twitter.com/RhianCahill
FaceBook – https://www.facebook.com/RhianCahillAuthor
Instagram – http://instagram.com/rhiancahill/
BookBub – https://www.bookbub.com/authors/rhian-cahill
Goodreads page - https://www.goodreads.com/rhian_cahill

LOOK FOR THESE TITLES BY RHIAN CAHILL

Coyote Hunger Series

Coyote Home – Book 1

Coyote Wild – Book 2

Coyote Whispers – Book 3

Coyote Law – Book 3.5

Coyote Lies – Book 4

Party Games Series

Truth Or Dare

Spin The Bottle

Pass The Parcel – Novella

Are You Game Series

7 Minutes In Heaven – Book 1

Catch'n'Kiss – Book 2

Red Light, Green Light – Book 3

Hearts Are Wild Series

No More Talking (novella)

Dare You To (novella)

Mad Love

For a full list of Rhian's available books visit her website

http://www.rhiancahill.com/books/